Happy Birthday, Cindy!

"What's going on?" Hannah asked. "You guys look awful."

"Where's the birthday girl? Where's Cindy?" Gil inquired. He gazed around the front room. "Let's get this party rolling!"

"The party's over," Gretchen moaned.

"Over?" Gil replied. "We haven't even cut the cake."

"It's Cindy—" Patrick began.

"Cindy is dead!" Gretchen blurted out. "Somebody killed her."

Hannah's arm fell away from Gil's waist. She took a step toward Gretchen.

"Huh? What did you say?" she asked slowly.

"Dead," Gretchen whispered. "Cindy is dead."

Don't miss these chilling tales from

FEAR STREET®

First Date

Secret Admirer

All-Night Party

The Confession

After hours, the horror continues at

FEAR STREET® NIGHTS

#1: Moonlight Secrets

#2: Midnight Games

#3: Darkest Dawn

R.L. STINE

FEAR STREET®

ALL-NIGHT PARTY

SIMON AND SCHUSTER

SIMON AND SCHUSTER
First published in Great Britain in 2006 by Simon & Schuster UK Ltd.
A CBS COMPANY
Africa House, 64-78 Kingsway, London WC2B 6AH

Previously published in the USA in 2005 by Simon Pulse,
an imprint of Simon & Schuster's Children's Division, New York.

Copyright © 1997 by Parachute Publishing, L.L.C.
FEAR STREET is a registered trademark of Parachute Press, Inc.

Designed by Sammy Yuen Jr.
The text for this book was set in Times.

A CIP catalogue record for this book is
available from the British Library

ISBN 1 416 91689 X
EAN 9781416916895

1 3 5 7 9 10 8 6 4 2

Printed by Cox & Wyman Ltd, Reading, Berks

ALL-NIGHT PARTY

"Tonight is going to be awesome!" Hannah Waters exclaimed. "Our plan is brilliant."

Gretchen Davies stopped her blue minivan at a red light, then turned to her best friend. "You think Cindy will be surprised?" she asked Hannah.

Hannah nodded, her green eyes sparkling. "She doesn't suspect a thing. She thinks we totally forgot her birthday. She sounded really upset when we all had excuses for not hanging out with her tonight. Especially since her parents had to go away on business this week."

"She's probably sitting around, pigging out on junk food and feeling sorry for herself," Hannah's boyfriend, Gil Shepherd, commented with a laugh.

"Little does she know, she's about to be kidnapped," Jackson Kane chimed in from the backseat.

"And dragged off for an all-night party on Fear Island," Gil added.

"It was so nice of your grandfather to let us use his cabin, Gil," Gretchen said. She glanced over her shoulder at Gil, who sat in the backseat between Jackson and their other friend, Patrick Munson.

"Yeah—a surprise party is one thing. But an overnight party in our own private cabin is totally cool," Patrick said.

"Definitely," Jackson agreed.

Gretchen nodded happily. It felt great to be part of the "kidnapping" plan—especially since she hadn't known Cindy as long as the others.

She had moved to Shadyside only six months before, when her dad's job transferred him here.

She expected it to be hard starting a new school her senior year. But Hannah had helped her fit right in and introduced her to all her friends.

"I've never done anything like this before," Gretchen confided.

Hannah snickered. "Neither have we. But it's exactly what Cindy deserves."

"Light's green," Jackson pointed out.

Gretchen shifted her eyes back to the road and started driving again. Six blocks later, she turned onto the street where Cindy lived.

Gretchen pulled her minivan up to a curb several houses away from Cindy's and turned off the engine.

"Does everyone know what they're supposed to do?" Patrick asked.

"I'm all set," Jackson replied. "How about you, Gretchen?"

Gretchen glanced in the rearview mirror. Her gaze met Jackson's. She felt a tiny shiver race up her back. She looked away.

She had hung out with Jackson since she moved to Shadyside, but she still didn't know him very well.

She wasn't sure why, but Jackson gave her the creeps.

When they first met, she thought he was sort of cute. But he seemed so moody. Serious and quiet.

Gretchen didn't think she'd ever seen him smile. Most of the time he stood apart from the group, watching everything.

Definitely a strange guy.

But weird enough to get his kicks making prank calls? Gretchen wondered.

For the last two weeks she'd been getting annoying hang-up calls. Always late at night, on the private line in her bedroom. Whenever she picked up the phone, the line went dead.

Only her friends had the number to that phone. So she figured it had to be somebody she knew.

And every time Gretchen caught Jackson watching her, she got a creepy feeling that he was the one.

One thing was for sure. He was always staring at her.

Like now. She could feel his dark brown eyes on her back.

Gretchen whirled around in her seat to face Patrick.

The movement must have caught Jackson off guard. With a guilty expression on his face, he tore his eyes away from her.

"We all know what to do," Gretchen told Patrick. "Let's go. Let's kidnap Cindy."

Gretchen gazed up at Cindy's house.

Cindy is going to be so surprised, she thought.

She glanced at Jackson and felt a sudden chill.

This is going to be a great party, she assured herself. Tonight is going to be so much fun.

So why did she suddenly have such a bad feeling?

chapter

2

"Let's get moving," Hannah urged, climbing out of the minivan.

Gretchen locked the driver's door as her friends piled out of the van.

Patrick led the way. Gretchen walked beside Hannah.

"This is perfect," Patrick murmured as they moved through the darkness.

Suddenly feeling nervous, Gretchen glanced around.

The street stood dark and deserted. She saw no lights on in any of the nearby houses.

A gust of wind whipped strands of her dark brown hair across her face. The moonless night sky carried the promise of an approaching storm.

"We'll be able to slip in and out," Patrick said with a chuckle. "We'll grab Cindy and disappear. No one will even know we were here."

They reached Cindy's house. Patrick signaled the others to follow him to the backyard.

A light above the back door cast long shadows across the grass. Gretchen spotted a single light on in the house. The second floor. Cindy's room.

Then she saw Hannah hunch down next to the back door and lift a potted plant from the cement step.

"Got it!" Hannah whispered.

She held up a door key.

A cold gust of wind cut across the porch, and Gretchen shivered. March really came in like a lion this year, Gretchen thought.

She hugged herself inside her denim jacket, wishing she'd worn a heavier coat.

She dug her hands deep into her pockets as she waited for Hannah to open the back door.

As Gretchen tucked a few strands of her hair behind her ears, she caught Jackson staring at her again.

What is his problem? she wondered.

She gave him a warm smile, hoping he would smile back at her.

But he didn't. He stared down at the ground, his lips twisted in a frown. Then he turned his back on her.

I don't get it, Gretchen thought. I try to be friendly

to him. But Jackson acts as if he doesn't want anything to do with me.

Okay, Jackson. Play it your way. But I'm done trying to be nice to you. You are one strange dude.

Hannah fumbled with the key. Finally, she managed to open the back door.

They all tiptoed into the dark kitchen. They huddled together for a minute, listening for the slightest sound, eyes searching the darkness.

Gretchen didn't hear a thing. Except for the ticking of a clock in the dining room. And the sounds of everyone else breathing.

"The coast is clear," Gil whispered.

"Let's head upstairs," Patrick instructed. "Cindy is probably in her room."

They crept out of the kitchen and down the hall. Up the front staircase.

At the top of the stairs, Gretchen could see a light underneath the door of Cindy's bedroom.

She was home.

Alone.

Unaware of what was about to happen.

Outside Cindy's bedroom door, Patrick placed a finger to his lips. Then, as they had planned, he began silently counting off on his fingers. *Five . . . four . . . three . . . two . . .*

When Patrick reached *one,* they burst into Cindy's bedroom.

The bedroom door slammed against the wall. To Gretchen, it sounded like a clap of thunder.

She saw Cindy sprawled across her bed reading a fashion magazine.

Cindy sprang up in surprise. She stared at them in shock.

"What's going on?" she demanded. "How did you get in? What are you doing here?"

Gil and Jackson pounced on her. They grabbed her arms and pulled her off the bed.

"Hey!" Cindy protested. "Let go! What are you *doing?*"

Cindy struggled to break free, but Gil and Jackson were too strong for her. They held her still while Gretchen and Hannah wrapped a blindfold around Cindy's eyes.

"This isn't funny, guys!" Cindy cried. "What's going on? What are you doing?"

"Hold still, Cindy. I don't want to hurt you," Gretchen said. She tightened the blindfold behind Cindy's head. "We'll explain later."

Gretchen stepped away from Cindy. She gave a sigh of relief.

So far, so good. Everything was going according to plan.

"Got the blindfold on, Patrick—" she began.

She turned to Patrick—and the rest of the words died in her throat.

Gretchen gasped. What was going on? This wasn't part of the plan!

Why was Patrick holding a pistol?

"Hey—!" she choked out. The silver barrel glistened as Patrick pointed the gun at Cindy.

"Hold still, Cindy," Patrick said, mimicking Gretchen's voice. "We don't want to hurt you."

With a nasty grin, he pressed the pistol into Cindy's side.

Cindy's shrill scream echoed through the silent house.

chapter

3

"Noooo!" Gretchen wailed. "Patrick—drop it!"

Had Patrick lost his mind?

Hannah dove forward and grabbed Patrick's arm. "Are you crazy? Put that down!" she screamed.

Patrick laughed. "Calm down!"

He jammed the gun back into the pocket of his black leather jacket. "It's gone."

"You never said anything about bringing a gun!" Gretchen cried in a trembling voice.

"No big deal. I thought it would make our kidnapping more realistic," Patrick explained. "You can check it out. It's not loaded or anything."

"What's going on?" Cindy demanded angrily. "Do

you really have a gun? What are you doing in my house?"

"We're kidnapping you," Gretchen told her.

"Huh? Kidnapping me? Why?"

"We're taking you away for an all-night birthday party!" Gretchen told her.

"You are?" Cindy squealed excitedly. "Where?"

"You'll have to wait and see," Gretchen instructed. She followed Gil and Jackson out of the bedroom.

They led Cindy down the front stairs. "That's why you're blindfolded," Hannah told her.

"You guys scared me to death," Cindy said, shaking her head. "You really did."

"That was the idea!" Gretchen laughed.

"Can't I take this blindfold off?" Cindy asked when they were all settled in the minivan. She reached up to pull off the blindfold.

"No way," Gretchen answered. "It stays on until we take it off."

"But I can't see anything!" Cindy protested.

"That's the whole point," Gil laughed.

"Cindy loves doing her helpless routine," Hannah grumbled, sliding into the front passenger seat.

"It works for her," Gretchen joked.

Hannah sighed. "No kidding."

Gretchen smiled uneasily, and started up the engine.

After all these months, she still hadn't figured out Hannah and Cindy's friendship. They were more like

11

rivals than friends, always competing for something. Grades. Attention. Boys.

When it came to boys, Cindy definitely had the edge over Hannah. Practically every guy at Shadyside High had a crush on Cindy.

Petite with big blue eyes and white-blond hair, she was the type of girl guys always fell for. Big time.

Boys just loved taking care of Cindy. That included Gil, who had been Cindy's boyfriend until they broke up at the end of last summer.

Gretchen turned to Hannah, who was fastening her seat belt. Tall and athletic, with freckles and a wild mass of red curls, Hannah didn't need anybody to take care of her.

"Why don't you turn on the radio?" Patrick suggested from the backseat. "If this is a party, we need some music, don't we?"

"I will if you answer a question for me," Gretchen replied, pulling the minivan away from the curb.

"Shoot," Patrick replied. Then he groaned. "Poor choice of words."

"I still can't believe you brought a gun along," Gretchen said. "Where did you get it? Why did you do it?"

Patrick hesitated.

Gretchen could sense there was something he wanted to confess, but was holding back. "What's wrong, Patrick? What's going on?" she demanded.

"I'm really not supposed to tell any of you this," he said finally. "The police are keeping it quiet."

12

"Keeping what quiet?" Hannah asked.

"Come on," Jackson urged. "You can tell us. We can keep a secret."

Patrick hesitated, staring out the van window. "No. I'd better not tell you," he said softly. "It could spoil the whole party."

"*T*ell us," Gretchen urged. "You can't keep us in suspense. You have to tell us now."

Patrick sighed. "My dad came to visit today," he began. "You know he's a police officer in Waynesbridge where he lives with his new wife."

Gretchen nodded. After his parents had divorced the year before, Patrick and his mother had moved from Waynesbridge to Shadyside. "What did your father tell you?"

"He told me that a prisoner escaped from the prison upstate," Patrick revealed. "He was spotted in the Fear Street Woods."

"Fear Street Woods!" Hannah gasped.

Patrick nodded. "I didn't bring the gun along for

14

the kidnapping. My dad gave it to me. Just in case we run into the prisoner on Fear Island."

"Patrick!" Hannah wailed. "You have such a big mouth! Now Cindy knows where we're taking her. You ruined the whole surprise."

"Oh, wow. I'm sorry," Patrick groaned.

"Never mind that," Cindy said, pulling off her blindfold. "Tell us more about the prisoner."

"What did he do?" Gretchen asked.

Patrick didn't answer.

Gretchen repeated her question. "Patrick, what did he *do?*"

Patrick shook his head. "You don't want to know. Trust me."

"Yes, I do. Tell us," Gretchen insisted.

"He murdered three girls. Teenagers," Patrick murmured softly.

"Whoa!" Hannah cried.

"How did he kill them?" Gretchen asked. She turned the minivan onto the gravel road that led through the woods to Fear Lake.

"Please!" Hannah protested. She covered her ears with her hands. "I really don't need to hear the gruesome details."

"I don't know how he killed them," Patrick admitted. "My dad didn't tell me. He only warned me to be careful."

"Why didn't you tell us all this before?" Gretchen asked. She parked the minivan near the shore. "We could have changed our plans."

15

"I promised my dad I wouldn't," Patrick explained. He sighed again. "I wish I hadn't taken the gun out when we were kidnapping Cindy! Then you wouldn't have known. And we all could have had a good time. Now I've ruined the party for everyone."

"Maybe we should go somewhere else," Hannah suggested tensely. "To play it safe."

"Hannah is right," Patrick agreed.

Gil shook his head. "No way. I'm not scared."

"Me either," Jackson chimed in. "Anyway, we worked so hard to fix up the cabin. All our stuff is already on Fear Island. We'd still have to go across the lake to get it."

"Why would a prisoner go to Fear Island?" Cindy asked. "He probably wants to put as much distance between himself and the police as he can. I'll bet he's in another state by now."

"The birthday girl has spoken!" Gil announced. Gretchen heard the van's side door slide open and saw Gil jump out. Hannah followed. Then Patrick, who helped Cindy out.

Gretchen suddenly found herself alone with Jackson.

"What about you, Gretchen?" Jackson asked. "Are you scared?"

Gretchen turned. She forced herself to stare into the depths of Jackson's dark eyes.

His words had sounded taunting. As if he were hoping she might be afraid. As if he were trying to frighten her.

"No, I'm not scared."

16

"I think you are," Jackson replied quietly.

Gretchen felt her throat clench with fear. "You're such a jerk, Jackson," she snapped. "The killer is not out there. Hiding on Fear Island makes no sense."

A smile twitched on Jackson's lips. "Don't say I didn't warn you."

Jackson's smile chilled Gretchen.

What is he saying? Is he *threatening* me? she wondered.

How twisted is he?

chapter
5

"Come on!" Patrick shouted. "We're wasting time. Let's party!"

After locking up the minivan, Gretchen followed the others to a dock at the lake shore. Gretchen spotted the rowboat that floated beside the dock on the dark water.

Patrick climbed aboard first. Then he helped Hannah down into the boat.

Gretchen shivered, burrowing deeper into her denim jacket. She couldn't wait till they got indoors again.

The wind felt damp on her skin, and thick clouds covered the night sky.

She didn't need a weather report to know that rain would soon be falling in buckets. Gretchen hoped they wouldn't be caught in the boat when the storm began.

She boarded the boat last. Hannah gave her a hand.

Gretchen saw only one seat left, between Jackson and Patrick. She sat down, then stared straight ahead, pressing her hands between her knees.

Across from her, Gil sat between Cindy and Hannah. Hannah pushed off from the dock, and Jackson and Patrick began rowing.

"I don't know about the rest of you, but I'm freezing," Cindy complained, her teeth chattering.

"We pulled you away so fast, we forgot your coat," Gretchen said fretfully.

"Here. You can wear this." Gil slipped off his jacket and draped it around Cindy's shoulders. "Feel better?"

"Mmm," Cindy sighed. "Thanks."

"If that's not enough, I know an even better way to warm you up!" Gil added with an evil grin.

Gretchen rolled her eyes. Gil was such an animal. She didn't know how Hannah put up with him.

Of course, Cindy was no better. She loved to wrap guys around her finger, to get them to do whatever she wanted. Gretchen hated to watch Gil—or any guy for that matter—turn into a drooling little puppy around Cindy.

But somebody else, she realized, hated it even more. Gretchen saw that Hannah was barely keeping her anger under control. It had to be hard having your boyfriend still be friends with his ex-girlfriend.

19

"Hey!" Patrick cried out suddenly. He stopped rowing. "What's that?"

"What?" Gretchen demanded.

"Something in the water!"

"How can you see anything?" Hannah asked. "It's pitch black out."

"I saw a fin!" Patrick cried. "Over there."

Jackson and Gil peered in the direction where Patrick was frantically pointing his finger.

Jackson raised an eyebrow. "A fin? In a lake? Give me a break."

"I don't see anything," Gil murmured.

"It's coming closer!" Patrick shouted. The boat started rocking from side to side as he hummed the theme from *Jaws*. "Dum-dum . . . dum-dum . . . dum-dum-dum-dum-dum-dum-dum-dum."

Jackson rolled his eyes. "That's really lame!"

"You're such a loser, Patrick!" Gil laughed.

Gretchen groaned. It was another one of Patrick's dumb jokes.

"Grow up," Hannah muttered.

Patrick shrugged. "Admit it. You fell for it—for a moment."

"So is this the entire guest list for my party?" Cindy asked. "Isn't somebody missing?"

"Like who?" Hannah asked.

"Gretchen knows who," Jackson sneered.

Gretchen felt totally confused. "I do?"

"You remember that tall guy with the long, black hair?" Cindy teased. "Your boyfriend? Marco?"

Marco. Gretchen felt her body grow tense.

"I didn't invite him," she answered sharply.

"How come?" Cindy pouted. "I like Marco. He's so cute."

"I'm trying to give him a hint," Gretchen explained. "Maybe if he finds out he wasn't invited to your party, we'll be history. Then she added, "If you want him, Cindy, he's all yours."

"I'm sorry you guys are breaking up. I thought everything was going great," Cindy said.

Gretchen dug her cold hands deeper into her pockets. "Not anymore."

She stared out at the black water. She didn't feel like talking about Marco Hughes anymore.

Couldn't Cindy take a hint?

Sure, Gretchen and Marco *seemed* to be doing okay. Marco was totally different from the guys Gretchen usually went out with. There was something *dangerous* about him, and Gretchen had been instantly attracted.

With his long, black hair and silver hoop earring, not to mention the motorcycle he rode, Marco was a rebel. And they really had fun.

At first.

But as the weeks went by, she realized he was too wild. He didn't care about rules. He didn't care about schoolwork or grades or other people.

And he had a terrible temper.

Everything had to be done *his* way. Or else. The littlest thing could send Marco into a rage.

21

Gretchen didn't like admitting it to herself, but she was a little bit afraid of Marco. She'd been trying to break up with him for weeks.

She even suggested that they see other people. But he wasn't getting the message.

"Can we not talk about Marco tonight?" Gretchen begged. "I want to have a good time."

"I won't mention his name again," Cindy promised. She made an X over her heart. "Cross my heart."

"Hope to die," Gretchen and Hannah finished together.

"There's the island!" Jackson announced.

When the boat neared the dock, Jackson hopped out and tied it up. Hannah climbed out next and gave Gretchen a hand. Then Gil and Patrick helped Cindy.

Standing on the dock, Gretchen listened to the slap of the waves against the wood pilings and the wind in the trees. She saw big gray boulders on the shoreline, and beyond them, a thick mist floated over the dark woods.

Gil clicked on a flashlight and led the way to a rock-strewn path in the woods. The path that led to his grandfather's cabin.

As she trudged along the rough path, Gretchen thought about the decorations in the cabin that she and Hannah had worked so hard on.

They had rowed over by themselves that afternoon to decorate the cabin and bake Cindy's birthday cake. Gretchen felt especially pleased with all the candles they'd arranged in the front room.

Then she remembered. She was supposed to run ahead and light the candles before the others came in. The cabin would look really awesome.

She hurried ahead of her friends and raced up the path into the dark, misty woods.

Behind her, someone called her name. "Gretchen! Wait up! Do you want me to walk with you?"

Jackson!

Walk alone in the woods with him? No way! The thought creeped her out.

"No thanks," she called back. "I can go faster by myself."

Gretchen ducked her head and kept moving.

The path grew steep. She gasped for breath and slowed her pace.

She heard the wind howl through the trees and saw the long bare branches above her tossing from side to side.

Dead leaves swirled along the ground. She blinked as fat raindrops splattered on her face and hair. They'd made it to the island just in time.

Gretchen spotted the cabin and ran up the wooden front steps to the covered porch. She took a deep breath. Made it.

But as she reached for the doorknob she heard a creaking sound. Something moved in the shadows on the porch.

She turned to the side and saw the two empty rocking chairs swaying to and fro. Invisible party crashers?

"No ghosts. Just the wind," Gretchen whispered to herself. She hurried inside.

Gretchen flung the front door open. She reached for the light switch along the wall and flipped it up.

No lights.

Gretchen stared into the darkness.

She jiggled the switch up and down. What's going on? she thought. It worked perfectly this afternoon.

She jiggled it some more, then gave up.

Gretchen took a few steps into the darkness. She didn't feel scared. She knew the floor plan by heart.

The door opened to the front room. The kitchen and a bathroom were to her right. A stairway near the kitchen door led to the second floor where there were two bedrooms and another bathroom.

Gretchen decided to find a candle. She walked deeper into the room.

What was that?

She stopped—and listened.

Silence. Then she heard it clearly.

A footstep.

Then another.

Gretchen wanted to run, but her legs suddenly felt like two cement blocks.

The slow, heavy footsteps moved closer.

Gretchen turned and stumbled toward the door.

A tall figure jumped out of the shadows behind her.

Strong arms reached out of the darkness and wrapped around her.

She opened her mouth to scream.

A rough hand covered her mouth, smothering the sound.

The arms pulled her close.

Squeezing hard. Harder.

I'm dead, she realized. He's going to kill me!

chapter
6

Gretchen gasped for air. She squirmed and struggled to break free. No—please! Please! she silently begged.

To her surprise, the hands released her.

Gretchen stumbled, then whirled around to face her attacker.

"You?" she gasped.

"Surprise!" he cried. "Aren't you happy to see me?"

Marco.

Gretchen's pounding heart slowed. She felt her body sag with relief.

"Hey, Gretch," Marco laughed. "Did I scare you?"

"Yes!" Gretchen shouted. She pounded his chest with both fists.

She felt her fear drain away, replaced by simmering anger. She had been looking forward to a night away from Marco. Now here he was, standing in front of her.

She pulled a box of matches out of her pocket and lit one of the candles.

"Hey—it was just a joke," Marco said.

"You nearly scared me to death," Gretchen snapped. "For your information, there's an escaped killer on the loose. He—he murdered three girls. I thought—"

Marco ran a hand through his long hair. "How was I supposed to know that?"

"The police are keeping it quiet," Gretchen told him.

"Then how did you find out?"

"Patrick found out from his father, who told him not to spread it around."

"You can't be angry at me for something I didn't know," he argued. He tried to pull Gretchen back into his arms, but she wriggled free.

Marco stared at her with a hurt expression. Then he folded his arms across his chest and sighed.

She couldn't help but notice the way his white T-shirt hugged his muscles or the way his blue jeans were molded to his legs.

Marco had a great body.

Most girls at Shadyside High would love to trade places with her, she knew. But she really didn't want to go out with him anymore.

27

She couldn't help it. It was just the way she felt.

Gretchen stepped away from him and shrugged off her jacket. She hung it on an oak coatrack near the front door. "How did you even know I'd be out here?" she asked.

"Your mom told me when I called your house tonight," Marco replied.

He leaned against the banister leading upstairs and gave Gretchen a sly smile.

"I hid my boat on the other side of the island so I could surprise you," Marco boasted. "You can't get away from me so easily, Gretchen. Don't you know that?"

Gretchen frowned.

Does he *know* that I want to break up with him? Has he figured it out?

Probably not. Marco is so vain . . .

She heard sounds at the door and saw the beam of Gil's flashlight against the front windows.

A few seconds later, her friends piled through the doorway into the cabin.

Hannah caught sight of Marco, then threw Gretchen a puzzled look.

Later, Gretchen mouthed.

"Marco's here?" Cindy squealed.

"You didn't think I'd miss your birthday, did you?" Marco grinned.

He threw open his arms and Cindy raced into them, giving him a hug.

"I bet I look like a mess," Cindy muttered, pushing back her hair.

Some mess, Gretchen thought. Cindy looked perfect as always.

"We wanted to light all the candles first," Hannah apologized.

"This place looks great!" Cindy raved.

"It does, doesn't it?" Gretchen agreed.

She and Hannah had spent three hours decorating. Streamers were strung from one end of the living room to the other. Silver foil stars hung on the walls, along with gold and pink balloons. A HAPPY BIRTHDAY banner was positioned over the fireplace.

Gretchen had scattered candles, all different colors and sizes, throughout the room. She quickly began lighting them.

She stepped past their sleeping bags, piled in one corner of the room. Gretchen didn't think they'd be doing much sleeping tonight.

They'd be too busy partying.

Gretchen lit the last candle and blew out the match. "There. Now everything is perfect."

"Happy Birthday, Cindy," Hannah cried.

Everyone gathered around Cindy. "Happy Birthday!"

Cindy gazed around the decorated room. "No one has ever done anything this nice for me before. I can't believe you all went to so much trouble to surprise me."

"Why not?" Gretchen asked. "You're our friend."

29

"This is the best birthday I've ever had," Cindy gushed. "I'll remember it as long as I live."

Later, after the horror began, Gretchen remembered Cindy's words.

"I'll remember it as long as I live."

chapter

7

"Let's not forget the presents!" Gil cried.

"Or the food!" Patrick chimed in. "I hope we brought enough. I'm starved."

"As usual," Hannah murmured.

"If we run out of food, we'll have to go hunting," Marco said.

"Hunting? What's to hunt? There are no animals on Fear Island," Gretchen told him.

"Sure there are," Gil responded. "Right, Patrick?"

Patrick nodded, his brown curls bouncing. "There are plenty of wild animals out there. Lurking in the shadows." He lowered his voice to a sinister tone. "Waiting to pounce and kill when you least expect it."

"There are not!" Cindy declared. She glanced around the room nervously, then asked in a tiny voice, "Are there?"

Gretchen playfully swatted Patrick's arm. "Stop trying to scare us."

Patrick threw up his arms. "Okay, okay. But that animal growling sound you just heard is my stomach."

"Yeah, let's eat!" Gil exclaimed, starting for the kitchen. "But first, everyone take your boots off. House rules. My grandmother will freak out if we get mud on the rugs."

Gretchen could see Jackson watching them all. Not saying anything. A serious, almost angry, expression on his face.

Why is he watching us like that? Gretchen wondered. She dumped her boots by the front door with the others.

Is Jackson studying us? Why isn't he joining in like everyone else?

If he doesn't want to be here, why did he bother to come at all?

"Aren't you coming into the kitchen, Jackson?" she asked.

"I'm going to start a fire," he replied curtly. "You know. For roasting the hot dogs."

In the kitchen, Gretchen helped Hannah empty the refrigerator while Gil, Patrick, Marco, and Cindy brought paper cups, plates, and napkins out into the living room.

Gretchen saw the canisters of flour and sugar they had used to bake Cindy's birthday cake. They still cluttered the kitchen counter. Dirty bowls and pans filled the sink.

"Wow. Look at all that. We really made a mess baking today," Gretchen observed.

"Don't worry about it," Hannah said. "Everyone will pitch in to clean up later."

Gretchen moved the canister of flour to one side so she could reach a bag of hot dog rolls. "I guess."

"So what's the deal with Marco?" Hannah asked, handing Gretchen a package of hot dogs. "I thought you didn't want him here tonight."

"He called my house, and my mom told him where I was."

Hannah made a face. "Oh, wow."

"It's not Mom's fault," Gretchen said. "She doesn't know I want to break up with him."

Hannah crammed her arms with bottles of ketchup, mustard, and pickles. "What are you going to do?"

Gretchen shrugged. "Try to keep my distance."

"Good luck. This cabin isn't very big, in case you didn't notice," Hannah reminded her.

"Yeah, I noticed." Gretchen sighed. She followed Hannah into the living room. "I'll have to make the best of it. It's only one night. How bad can it be?"

* * *

As Gretchen walked into the living room, she saw the fire blazing in the hearth. Gil handed out skewers for roasting the hot dogs.

Gretchen cooked her hot dog in the fire. Then she looked around for a place to eat.

She spotted Marco sitting on the floor next to Cindy. So Gretchen took a seat on the couch. But he instantly got up and sat down next to her.

Gretchen felt trapped.

She had a feeling that if she got up and sat on the floor, or even escaped to the kitchen, Marco would follow her.

He tried to put his arm around her shoulders. But she jumped up to get another soda.

I used to love when Marco put his arms around me, Gretchen remembered. I used to love when he hugged me. When he kissed me.

Now I don't want him to touch me ever again. I only want him out of my life.

"Anyone want another hot dog?" Cindy asked. She held out a hot dog that she had just finished roasting.

"I'll take another one," Gil called out. He held out his plate. "Hmmm. Looks good. What a chef."

"Thanks," Cindy replied with a sweet smile.

"And the hot dog looks pretty good, too," Gil added, laughing.

Cindy giggled.

Gretchen felt as if she were going to gag on her food. She sneaked a glance at Hannah. Hannah sat staring at Gil, her mouth set in a tight line.

"You want some mustard and sauerkraut?" Cindy asked Gil.

"Gil doesn't like mustard on his hot dog," Hannah cut in. "He likes ketchup."

"No, he doesn't," Cindy insisted. "He likes mustard, don't you, Gil?"

Gil didn't answer either Cindy or Hannah. He grabbed the hot dog and took a bite. "It's fine just the way it is," he replied.

Hannah leaned over and reached into a cooler for a can of Coke. She popped the can open and handed it to Gil. "Have a soda."

Cindy shook her head. "Gil doesn't like Coke. He likes ginger ale."

"He does not."

"I should know, Hannah," Cindy replied smugly. "Gil and I went out for six months and you've only been going with him for one."

Gretchen could see that Cindy's remark was like a slap in the face to Hannah. Hannah left Gil's side and stormed into the kitchen.

Gretchen hurried after her. She found Hannah by the sink. She could see Hannah was upset. Her whole body was trembling.

"Don't let Cindy get to you," Gretchen advised. "She's just jealous because Gil's going out with you now."

"I've known Cindy all my life and sometimes I hate her so much," Hannah said through gritted teeth. "She thinks because she's pretty and blond, she can get everything she wants. It's not fair, Gretchen. It's just not fair!"

"You're not upset because Cindy is flirting with Gil, are you? There's something else."

"Yes," Hannah reluctantly admitted.

"Want to tell me?"

"Cindy won the college scholarship I applied for," Hannah whispered.

Gretchen's heart ached for Hannah. She knew how much Hannah had been relying on that scholarship.

For weeks she'd been on pins and needles waiting to hear if she'd won it.

"I'm sorry," Gretchen said softly.

Hannah turned away from the sink, facing Gretchen. "Her father has loads of money. He can afford to send her to any college she wants to go to. My parents can't. That scholarship was my only chance!"

"But didn't you apply for other scholarships?"

"That's not the point!" Hannah snapped. "Cindy wasn't even interested in that scholarship until she heard I was applying for it. It's been that way ever since we were kids."

Hannah uttered an angry sigh. "Cindy thinks she can get whatever she wants, no matter who she hurts. Well, she can't! Sometimes I wish she was dead!"

Gretchen gasped. She had never seen Hannah so angry.

Hannah was always so warm and sensitive. She

never said mean things about people—even when they deserved it.

But staring at Hannah now, Gretchen felt a chill. Her friend's face was a mask of bitter anger.

"You don't mean that," Gretchen whispered.

Hannah sighed. "Don't I? Don't I?"

chapter

8

*"H*ey, did you guys get lost in the kitchen or something?" Patrick cried as Gretchen and Hannah returned to the front room. "We thought we were going to have to send out a search team."

"So, what's next?" Marco asked.

"It's time to open my presents!" Cindy gleefully announced.

"There they are." Patrick pointed to the pile of gifts near the fireplace. "Go for it."

Cindy hurried over to the presents. Gretchen took a seat on the couch to get a good view.

Gretchen watched her pick a small box wrapped in pink foil from the top of the pile and shake it. Then Cindy tore off the gift card and read it aloud. "From

Gretchen," she announced. "Let's see. What could this be?"

She ripped off the paper and opened the box. "Great earrings. Thanks, Gretchen," she called out.

Before Gretchen could reply, Cindy tossed the box aside and was eagerly opening her next gift. A bottle of perfume from Hannah.

"I love this perfume. Too bad it makes me break out," she said.

She grabbed up the next present from Gil and Jackson. An envelope containing two tickets to a rock concert.

Everybody Gretchen knew was dying to see that show. But Cindy didn't look too excited about it. "Hey, thanks, guys. Cool gift," Cindy said. She dropped the tickets on top of her present pile.

Cindy is so self-centered and spoiled, Gretchen thought as she watched Cindy tear open her gifts. Everyone put a lot of time and thought into her presents, and she doesn't even appreciate it.

"Hey, Cindy! I'm real sorry!" Patrick suddenly said. "I forgot to wrap your gift. I'll have to give it to you later, okay?"

"Sure." Cindy shrugged. She reached for the last box. A large white one.

Gretchen watched Cindy shake the large box. She noticed that there wasn't any paper on the outside. Just a red stick-on bow on top.

Gretchen read the words scrawled on the top of the box in black marker: "To Cindy. From Marco."

"The last present is yours," Cindy told Marco as she shook the box. "I wonder what it is."

"Open it and see," he encouraged.

Cindy ripped off the red bow and lifted the lid of the box. She peeked inside—and her mouth dropped open in disgust.

"Ohhhh. Gross!" she moaned.

chapter

9

"Yuck!" Cindy made a disgusted face.

"Hey, you're welcome," Marco laughed. "If you don't like them, I'll take them back."

Cindy turned to Gretchen and Hannah. "He gave me a bunch of slasher movies," she announced. She picked a videotape out of the box and read the title. *"Bloodfest 4."*

Gretchen stared at the video. The cover had a picture of a half-dressed girl shrinking away from a long dagger, dripping blood.

Cindy groaned and made a face. "Ugh! How can any *normal* person watch that stuff?"

Gretchen just shrugged. She couldn't believe how rude Cindy was being. Why couldn't she pretend to like Marco's gift instead of hurting his feelings?

"If you don't want the videos, can I have them?" Patrick asked. "I'll add them to my collection."

Cindy waved a hand. "They're yours."

"I don't believe her," Marco muttered, shaking his head.

Gretchen glanced around the room at her friends. Everyone looked sort of down. And this was supposed to be a great night. Their awesome all-night party.

"How about some music?" Gretchen suggested. "It's way too quiet in here!"

"Good idea. Let's crank it up. There's no one around to complain," Gil said.

Gretchen inserted a CD into the portable CD player and turned the volume as high as it would go. A heavy rock-and-roll beat filled the room. She felt the wooden floorboards vibrating under her feet.

"Excellent!" Hannah cried over the noise. She grabbed Gil by the hand and pulled him up to dance.

"Come on, Gretchen," Marco urged.

"I don't feel like it. Maybe later," Gretchen stammered. "I feel sort of tired," she added.

"Tired?" Marco cried. "You can't be tired. This is an all-night party!"

Before Gretchen could refuse again, Marco took her by the arm and started dancing. Gretchen gave up and started to dance, too.

As they danced, Gretchen could see Cindy's eyes locked on Gil and Hannah. Gil was whispering in her ear and Hannah had a smile on her face.

Gretchen wondered if Cindy was sorry she had

broken up with Gil. She knew that Cindy had been the one to drop him.

It happened because Gil got into serious trouble. Some guys he used to hang out with decided to steal a car.

Cindy's parents went ballistic when they found out. A few days later, Cindy broke up with Gil.

After that, Gil and Hannah started going out.

Gretchen couldn't understand Hannah's attraction to Gil. Sure, he was cute enough, with his high cheekbones, blue eyes, and jet-black hair.

But he wasn't such a prize. Who wanted a boyfriend who was constantly coming on to his ex-girlfriend?

Gretchen's eyes drifted away from Gil and Hannah. Patrick was stuffing his face with another hot dog.

Jackson leaned against the wall next to the fireplace. His arms were crossed over his chest.

His dark eyes were riveted on her.

Watching.

Following her every move.

chapter
_____

10

The song ended. Gretchen pulled away from Marco.

"I'm going outside to get some more wood for the fire," she said.

"Want some help?" he offered.

Gretchen knew if Marco tagged along, they wouldn't be gathering wood. He'd want the two of them to find a private spot and make out.

The thought made her stomach knot.

"No thanks," Gretchen replied. What she really wanted was to get away from Marco—and Jackson— for a while.

She was really beginning to feel trapped inside the little cabin.

Grabbing a flashlight off the fireplace mantel, Gretchen headed for the door. She could feel Jackson's gaze following her, but she didn't turn around.

"We'll walk out with you," Hannah called. "Gil and I are going down to the boat dock to look at the stars."

Gretchen rolled her eyes. Who did Hannah think she was fooling?

There weren't any stars out. It was so obvious. She and Gil were going to make out.

"I'm not budging an inch," Patrick sighed from the couch. "I ate too many hot dogs." He burped loudly.

"Better make room for dessert," Hannah said. "We're going to cut Cindy's birthday cake when we get back."

"Do you know what you're going to wish for?" Gretchen asked Cindy.

Cindy stared at Gil with determination. "I know exactly what I'm going to wish for."

"Be careful what you wish for," Gil replied. "You just might get it."

Cindy smiled coyly. "I'll take that chance."

Hannah tugged impatiently on Gil's arm. "Come on, Gil. Let's go."

After lacing up her hiking boots, Gretchen snagged her denim jacket from the coatrack. She slipped into it and stepped onto the porch.

Gretchen took a deep breath. She felt surrounded

by the night's deep, velvety silence. So peaceful. So quiet. So different from inside the cabin.

She suddenly wished she didn't have to go back.

Back to Marco.

Back to Jackson.

Gretchen stared up at the sky. It had stopped raining, but thick clouds still hovered above. Another storm was approaching.

I'd better get the firewood before it starts raining again, she thought.

Clicking on her flashlight, Gretchen hurried down the porch steps and made her way alongside the cabin to a nearby shed. She found a few pieces of wood inside and picked them up.

As she approached the back of the cabin, she heard loud voices. From in the kitchen.

Gretchen felt embarrassed eavesdropping. But she couldn't resist.

She moved closer to the cabin wall and stood just below the kitchen window.

She couldn't see inside. The window was too high. But she heard the voices clearly.

Two voices.

Male and female.

Raised and angry.

She recognized Cindy's voice. But who was the boy?

She listened more closely.

Jackson.

But what could *they* be arguing about? Cindy

46

and Jackson were only casual friends—weren't they?

Gretchen listened hard. She couldn't make out any words, but the argument sounded angry.

Then she heard a sharp sound that made her gasp in surprise.

A slap.

chapter

11

Was it a slap?

Yes. Cindy cried out.

Alarmed, Gretchen lurched away from the window.

What should she do? Go back inside and check it out?

No. It wasn't any of her business.

Besides, Patrick and Marco were still inside. If things got out of control between Cindy and Jackson, one of them would break it up.

Gretchen hurried away from the cabin. With the beam from her flashlight leading the way, she moved deeper into the forest, needing a little more time away from everyone.

As she walked on, the light flickered and grew dim. She could barely see the trees in front of her.

Oh, no, Gretchen thought. The flashlight is dying.

She shook the flashlight until the batteries rattled. The beam of light grew strong again, and Gretchen sighed with relief.

I guess I'd better head back for the cabin. I don't want to get caught out here in the dark with no way of finding my way back.

But before Gretchen could turn around, the light went out.

"Great," Gretchen muttered.

She flicked the switch back and forth. She jiggled the batteries.

Nothing happened.

Gretchen sighed. She tried not to panic.

Ever since she was a little girl, she had been afraid of the dark.

Afraid of something lurking in the shadows.

Waiting.

Watching.

Stop it! she scolded herself. Stop scaring yourself.

Still, Gretchen didn't like being by herself.

Especially with an escaped prisoner on the loose.

She turned and started walking back in the darkness.

As she walked, Gretchen listened to the sounds of the forest. The hooting of an owl. The chirping of crickets.

Then, far up ahead, through the trembling branches, Gretchen could see the lights from the cabin.

Okay, it's not so far. I can make it.

Then she heard something else.

A scraping sound.

Up ahead of her.

Gretchen stopped. "Who's there?" she called out.

No answer.

"Is anyone there?" she called again.

Still no answer.

"Marco, if that's you, I don't think it's funny," Gretchen called into the darkness.

No answer.

The scraping grew louder.

Gretchen felt her body trembling with fear. She held her breath and listened.

Something was out there.

Coming closer.

The sound vanished. Gretchen's body sagged in relief. She took a gulp of air.

No one's there. I'm freaking out over nothing. It was only an animal. That's all.

She searched for the cabin lights again. But she couldn't see them through the thick brush.

It's out there, somewhere, she reassured herself. I know it.

She took a few steps forward, but stopped when another sound ripped through the silence of the night.

The sound of *breathing*.

Human breathing.

"Who's there?" Gretchen cried out.

No answer.

But the breathing grew heavier.

Gretchen's mouth turned dry. She stopped and

leaned against a tree trunk. She could feel her heart pounding against her ribs.

If it was Hannah or Gil or anyone else from the cabin, they'd answer.

Unless . . .

Unless it *wasn't* someone from the cabin.

And if it wasn't one of her friends . . .

Gretchen's stomach tightened as she realized who it might be.

The escaped prisoner.

I've got to run, she decided. But before she could move, a figure leapt out of the woods.

And grabbed her.

chapter

12

Gretchen opened her mouth to scream, but no sound came out.

Marco laughed.

"Gotcha again!" he exclaimed, holding her tightly.

"You idiot!" Gretchen shrieked.

She furiously pounded her fists on his chest. "You're sick! You're really sick!"

"Whoa—calm down," Marco protested. "It was only a joke."

"Joke? I *told* you about the escaped prisoner! What were you thinking?"

"Gretchen, lighten up."

"Let me go!" Gretchen cried, struggling to break away from him. "Let me go!"

Marco dropped his arms and backed away. "What's

your problem? All night long you've been avoiding me. You act as if you don't even want me here."

"I *don't!*" Gretchen blurted out.

"Huh?"

"You weren't supposed to be here. I purposely didn't invite you," she admitted.

Marco's face grew tight as he stared at Gretchen. She'd seen that expression before. Right before he lost his temper.

Gretchen braced herself and watched his reaction.

"What did I do?" Marco asked.

"Nothing," Gretchen replied, shaking her head. "It's just that—" She stopped. She didn't know how to explain.

But she had to tell him. "Listen, I didn't invite you because I didn't want to see you. I guess I don't want to see you anymore."

"Huh?" Marco took a step toward Gretchen. She backed away from him.

"What's the matter, Gretchen?" Marco asked. He sneered at her. "Scared of me?"

"No. No, I'm not," she replied, taking another step back.

His hand reached into the back pocket of his jeans. He pulled out a slim, shiny metal object.

Her eyes widened with shock and her breath caught in her throat.

A switchblade glistened in the palm of his hand.

Marco pressed a button, and the blade snapped out.

"What are you doing with that thing?" Gretchen cried. "Put it away."

"I need it," Marco answered quietly. "I need it."

Gretchen inched away from Marco. She tried not to stare at the knife in his hand. But she couldn't tear her eyes away.

"I didn't mean to hurt you, Marco," Gretchen whispered. "Honest. Maybe I'm not so good at explaining these things. But we're not right for each other. Can't you see?"

Marco didn't answer. He moved closer to Gretchen.

"I've used this knife before, and I'm going to use it again," he whispered. "Tonight."

Tonight?

"Marco—no!" Gretchen shrieked.

Marco swung his hand up high.

And plunged the knife into Gretchen's chest.

chapter
13

With a groan, Gretchen shut her eyes and waited for the stab of pain.

Her hands shot up to her chest.

She felt nothing. Nothing at all.

A sharp, slicing sound made her open her eyes.

"Ohh!" she cried out, realizing that Marco hadn't stabbed her.

He had stabbed the switchblade into the bark of a tree behind her.

Gretchen spun around and watched the knife tear through the soft wood.

Once. Twice. Three times.

She froze, unable to move a muscle as Marco savagely hacked away at the tree.

Bits of damp bark hit her face. Marco was grunting and gasping for breath as he slashed at the tree.

"W-w-what are you doing?" Gretchen stammered.

"I'm angry," Marco shot back through gritted teeth. "I'm really angry, Gretchen. I—I don't understand. Why did you do this to me?"

"I'm sorry," Gretchen stammered. She bit down on her lower lip. "I don't know what else to say."

Marco stepped back from the tree, breathing heavily. He wiped sweat off his forehead with the back of his hand. Then he closed the knife and slid it back into his pocket.

Without saying another word, Marco turned his back on Gretchen and walked toward the cabin.

Gretchen hurried after him. She didn't know what she was going to say when she caught up. But she could see that she had hurt his feelings.

She hadn't meant to be so blunt, but . . .

"Marco—" she began.

He cut her off. "Save it, Gretchen. You got your message across. Loud and clear."

They walked the rest of the way in silence. As they neared the cabin, it started raining again, cold, heavy drops.

Gretchen opened the door of the cabin, expecting to hear laughter and voices.

But she heard only silence.

She stepped into the front room. The fire had burned low. Some of the candles had gone out. The birthday banner draped over the fireplace had fallen.

A chill swept down Gretchen's spine. The emptiness of the room spooked her.

"Where is everyone?" she wondered.

Marco shrugged. "Maybe they went out for a walk. Or maybe they went home. Some party."

Marco flopped down on the sofa, his arms crossed over his chest. He stared into the low flames of the dying fire.

Gretchen listened to the rain beat steadily on the cabin roof. Within seconds, everyone would be rushing inside, ready to party.

I'd better go get the cake set up, she thought.

Gretchen pushed open the kitchen door.

She stopped in alarm. What a mess! What had happened in here?

The canister of flour on the counter had been tipped over, spilling flour everywhere.

On the floor. On the counter.

But what were those stains in the flour?

Dark red stains.

Gretchen's eyes followed the dark trail.

"No!" She uttered a sharp cry when she saw Cindy.

On the floor.

On her back in the flour.

An angry red slash in her side.

Blood leaked out, over her clothes, forming a dark puddle in the white flour.

Cindy.

In the flour.
White and red. Dark, dark red.
Cindy.
A lifeless, blank stare on her face.
Her mouth locked open in a scream of horror and pain.

chapter

14

Gretchen staggered against the wall. She clutched her stomach.

I feel so sick, she thought. She fell to her knees and started to vomit.

Her stomach heaved. Then, wiping a hand across her mouth, she tore her eyes away from Cindy's body and ran out of the kitchen in a panic.

How did this happen? Where is everyone?

A few steps from the kitchen door, she stumbled into Marco. He caught her in his arms.

"Gretchen—what?" Marco demanded.

"It—it's Cindy," Gretchen choked out. "She's been—someone has—"

"Huh? What about Cindy?" Marco demanded.

Gretchen tried to force the words out, but her

tongue felt like rubber. Hot tears rolled down her face. She squeezed her eyes shut. But she kept seeing Cindy's body.

The blood leaking from the open wound.

The red blood. The white flour.

Cindy's horrible, lifeless stare.

Murdered! Gretchen's mind shrieked. Cindy has been murdered! Someone I know has been murdered!

She looked up to see Patrick race out of the downstairs bathroom. "What's going on? What's wrong?"

"She's in there!" Gretchen choked out. "Go and see!"

She grabbed Patrick's arm. And started to tug him into the kitchen.

But she stopped when she saw the stain on Patrick's T-shirt.

"No!" Gretchen gasped. "No!"

The front of Patrick's shirt was covered in blood.

chapter
15

Gretchen felt the room spinning. A blackness closed in on her. I'm going to faint, she thought. She reached out to one of the walls for support.

Patrick killed Cindy! Gretchen's mind screamed. He killed her!

"How did you get that blood on your shirt?" Gretchen demanded.

Patrick stared down at his shirt. "I cut my hand trying to open the bedroom window upstairs," he answered.

He held up his bandaged right palm.

Was Patrick telling the truth? Gretchen couldn't think about that now.

"The kitchen," she whispered.

Marco dashed into the kitchen. But Patrick stayed by Gretchen's side.

Why isn't he running with Marco into the kitchen? Gretchen wondered.

Is it because he already knows what's in there?

"Gretchen? Maybe you should sit down or something. You look awful," Patrick said softly.

He reached out to touch her arm.

She flinched and pulled away. Her gaze dropped again to the bloodstains on his shirt.

Gretchen couldn't answer. Tears filled her eyes and blurred her vision. She blinked them away.

"The escaped prisoner," Patrick whispered, his eyes widening with fear. "How did he get in? Why did he kill Cindy?"

Gretchen heard a floorboard creak. She gasped in terror. She heard Patrick gasp, too, as he turned quickly toward the sound.

Then she heard familiar voices. Gil's and Hannah's voices.

They strolled into the cabin, arms around each other.

"What's going on?" Hannah asked. "You guys look awful."

"Where's the birthday girl?" Gil inquired. He gazed around the front room. "Let's get this party rolling!"

"The party's over," Gretchen moaned.

"Over?" Gil replied. "We haven't even cut the cake."

"It's Cindy—" Patrick began.

62

"Cindy is dead!" Gretchen blurted out. "Somebody killed her."

Hannah's arm fell away from Gil's waist. She took a step toward Gretchen.

"Huh? What did you say?" she asked slowly.

"Dead," Gretchen whispered. "Cindy is dead."

Hannah shook her head back and forth. "She can't be!" she whispered. "What are you saying?"

"It's true," Gretchen choked out.

Hannah's lower lip started to tremble and her eyes filled with tears. "Cindy can't be dead. She can't!" she sobbed.

Gil gaped at Gretchen in shock. "Are you sure?"

Gretchen nodded her head. "Her body's in the kitchen."

"What are we going to do?" Hannah sobbed. "What are we going to do?"

"We've got to get the police," Gretchen said.

"We *can't* get the police," Patrick cried.

Gretchen spun around to face him. She felt her feelings well up inside, as if she might explode.

Patrick always acted like such a know-it-all. Even at a time like this.

"Why not?" she demanded. "Cindy's been murdered! We have to do something!"

Patrick didn't answer.

He stepped quickly toward Gretchen, an intense look on his face.

What is he going to do? Gretchen wondered.

Is it because I mentioned the police?

Her eyes fell to the front of Patrick's shirt again.

To the blood.

Did he lie? Is that really Cindy's blood and not his?
Is he the killer?

Before she could back away, Patrick grabbed her.
His strong arms wrapped around her.

"Patrick—stop! What are you doing?" she cried.

chapter
16

*P*atrick drew Gretchen close to him.

He's hugging me, Gretchen realized. Patrick is only hugging me. He's not hurting me.

"Calm down, Gretchen," he whispered soothingly. "Calm down. We have to think clearly. We can't call the police. There isn't a phone in the cabin. There aren't any phones on Fear Island."

"Then we'll go home!" Gretchen cried. "We'll row back to Shadyside and get the police."

"We can't," Patrick insisted.

"Why not?" Gil asked.

"Because of the storm," Hannah said.

"And because of the killer," Patrick added. "He was in our kitchen. He might still be outside the cabin. We're safer inside. At least we have the gun. And he can't sneak up on us."

Gretchen pulled away from Patrick. She felt a little bit calmer.

Yes, the killer, she thought. We have to protect ourselves from the killer.

"But the gun isn't loaded," Hannah pointed out.

"I brought bullets," Patrick answered.

"Huh? You did?" Gil asked.

Patrick nodded his head. "I told you. My dad wanted to make sure we were safe."

He turned back to Gretchen. "Are you okay?"

No, I'm not okay! Gretchen wanted to scream. One of my closest friends is dead in the kitchen. She's been stabbed to death, and she's lying in a pool of blood.

But Gretchen didn't scream. She hugged her arms around her body.

She wanted to scream and cry. But she couldn't.

What would it accomplish? Cindy would still be dead.

If only I had rushed back into the cabin when I overheard that argument, she thought miserably. Maybe I could have prevented Cindy's murder.

"What's going on?" Jackson appeared in the doorway of the cabin with an armload of wood.

"Cindy's been murdered," Gretchen murmured.

She watched Jackson closely, waiting for his reaction.

But he didn't react at all. He didn't even blink.

He dropped the wood into the bin next to the

fireplace. Then he took off his yellow rain slicker and hung it on the coatrack.

What's wrong with him? Gretchen wondered. Doesn't he have any feelings?

"Don't you have anything to say?" Gretchen cried. "Didn't you hear me? Cindy's been murdered."

"This is a joke—right?" he asked.

"A joke?" Gretchen gasped.

Hannah shook her head sadly. "It's no joke, Jackson."

"In—in the kitchen," Gretchen murmured.

Jackson stared hard at them. Then he strode across the living room and threw open the kitchen door.

Everyone followed him. Except Gretchen. She stayed behind. She didn't want to see Cindy's lifeless body again.

But being alone in the empty living room frightened her.

She hurried into the kitchen—and saw Marco standing over Cindy's body. His face was deathly white.

Jackson and Patrick stood beside Marco, in shocked silence.

Gil and Hannah stood on the other side of Cindy's body. Hannah turned and buried her face in Gil's chest.

"Who could have done such a thing to Cindy?" Hannah sobbed. "Who?"

"It's really true," Gil whispered numbly. "She's really dead."

Hannah pulled her tear-stained face away from Gil's shirt. "We have to get to the police. Our parents. *Do* something."

"Hannah's right," Gretchen said. "We need help. If we all stay together, we can make it down to the boat dock. The escaped prisoner isn't going to attack all of us at once."

"It's too big a risk," Patrick insisted. "We only have to stay here until tomorrow afternoon. When we don't come home in the morning, our parents will send the police to look for us."

"What are we supposed to do in the meantime?" Hannah demanded shrilly. "I can't stay here now. I just can't!"

She began to sob again. Gil put his arms around her.

"I think we should try to get out of here," Gil said. "None of us wants to stay here with Cindy dead in the kitchen."

"If you want to risk your lives, go ahead," Patrick said. "But I'm not setting foot outside this cabin."

"But, Patrick—" Gretchen started.

"The escaped prisoner is a maniac!" Patrick cried. "He's already killed once tonight!"

Gretchen stared at Cindy's lifeless body. At the puddles of blood in the flour.

She imagined the way Cindy fought her killer. Struggled for her life.

Patrick is right, she decided.

The killer could be anywhere. We can't take such a dangerous risk.

68

"I don't want to die," Gretchen blurted out, trembling.

"Then let's all stay put," Patrick urged.

"Wait a minute," Hannah spoke up. "What if the prisoner isn't outside?"

"Where else would he be?" Gil asked.

"What if he's *inside?*"

chapter

17

"What if we're wrong?" Hannah demanded. "What if he's still inside, watching *us?*"

They all stared at her, thinking about her words.

"Maybe he didn't have a chance to get away after he murdered Cindy," Hannah continued. Her eyes darted around nervously. "Maybe he heard one of us coming back to the cabin and decided to hide."

"If he's inside the cabin," Patrick murmured, "then nobody is safe."

Marco looked around the kitchen uneasily. "We're sitting ducks."

"Patrick, where's your gun?" Gil asked. "Go get it."

"No!" Jackson ordered. "Don't take the gun out, Patrick."

"Why not?" Patrick demanded. "We need protection!"

"We don't know if the killer is inside," Jackson insisted. "Let's not jump to conclusions."

Hannah ignored Jackson's words and clutched Gil's arm. "Maybe he's in one of the closets, watching through a crack. Listening to everything we say."

"There's only one way to know for sure," Patrick said. "Search the cabin."

"We won't sleep tonight unless we know he's not inside," Marco said grimly.

Hannah shuddered. "I'm not going to be able to sleep tonight. Not with Cindy dead in the kitchen!"

"I'll search with you, Hannah," Gretchen volunteered.

Hannah wiped away her tears and gave Gretchen a grateful smile. "Thanks."

The guys began climbing the stairs to the second floor. Gretchen and Hannah tackled the first floor.

"Gretchen, I'm so scared," Hannah whimpered.

Gretchen reached for a knob on a closet door. She gazed over her shoulder at Hannah. "You're not the only one," she confessed.

Gretchen's sweaty palm slipped off the brass doorknob. She reached for it a second time and tightened her grip. Twisting the knob, she flung the door open.

The closet was filled with old clothes. No one hiding inside.

As Hannah hovered behind her, Gretchen opened the rest of the closets and peeked behind the drapes in the living room.

Each time, she braced herself for an attack.

Each time, they found no one.

Finally, there was only one place left to search.

The kitchen.

"I can't go back in there," Hannah cried. "I can't bear to see Cindy dead."

Gretchen paused with her hand on the kitchen door. "I'll go in by myself. You stay out here."

"No!" Hannah cried. "Don't leave me alone."

Gretchen sighed and took Hannah by the arm. She led her into the living room and sat her on the couch. "I won't leave you alone, Hannah. We'll ask one of the guys to search the kitchen."

Gretchen heard doors opening and closing upstairs. She kept waiting to hear a shout of discovery. But it never came.

"No killer. No killer," Hannah chanted. She pulled her knees up to her chest and started rocking back and forth.

"No killer inside," Gretchen repeated softly.

Hannah shivered. "I'm so cold."

"The fire has almost gone out," Gretchen said. "I'll build it back up."

Gretchen reached into the wood bin and tossed logs into the fire. Soon the flames started to grow, crackling and popping, and warm rays of heat drifted out of the fireplace.

Hannah climbed up from the couch and stood in front of the fire, holding out her hands.

"Better?" Gretchen asked.

"A little," Hannah replied.

Rain pounded the windowpane.

Gretchen stared out at the storm. Were they safe? Or was the escaped prisoner hiding out in the woods? Watching the cabin and getting ready to make his next move?

Would they get off the island alive?

Gretchen went to check the locks on the windows. Pushing aside the half-open drapes, she checked each window. All were secure.

But as the drapes fell back into place, Gretchen froze.

Something on the porch!

Something *moving!*

"Someone is out there!" Gretchen gasped.

chapter

18

Gretchen raced over to the wood bin and pulled out a heavy log.

"Who is it?" Hannah cried. "What did you see?"

Gretchen didn't answer. She ran to the door.

"You can't go out by yourself!" Hannah shrieked. "It's too dangerous! Let one of the guys check."

Gretchen reached for the doorknob. "By the time they get down here, he could be gone."

"Don't do this, Gretchen!" Hannah begged. "Please!"

Gretchen pulled open the front door. Lightning flashed across the sky. Rain fell in heavy sheets.

Gretchen slipped out onto the porch. She raised the heavy log in her hand.

Her eyes darted from side to side, seeking the

slightest movement. The wind sprayed her with rain. She felt her wet clothes sticking to her body.

Is my mind playing tricks on me? Gretchen wondered. Am I seeing things?

Over the pounding rain, Gretchen heard a sound. *Behind* her.

Before Gretchen could turn around, a hand fell heavily on her shoulder.

Gretchen whirled around, swinging the log in her upraised hand.

She stared into the eyes of her attacker.

The log fell from her hand and clattered to the porch floor.

Jackson.

"What are you doing out here by yourself?" he angrily demanded.

"When I checked the locks on the windows, I thought I saw someone out here. I was taking a look around."

"By yourself?" He scowled at her.

"Someone had to check things out," she replied.

"That was stupid, Gretchen," Jackson scolded. "You should have waited for one of the guys to go with you."

Gretchen didn't feel like arguing with him. She brushed past him and stepped back into the house.

Gretchen found a towel in the bathroom and dried herself off. Then she bundled herself in a yellow blanket and stood in front of the fireplace.

Her soaking-wet hair felt plastered to her head and

she tried to pull a comb through the tangles. Jackson stood beside her, wrapped in a blanket of his own, also warming himself up.

"He could have been watching you the entire time, getting ready to strike," Jackson said. "It's a good thing Hannah told me you were out there."

Jackson's words chilled Gretchen more than the icy rain outside. She recalled the scene in the kitchen that she'd overheard. Jackson and Cindy arguing.

The sound of the slap.

Then the silence.

Should she ask Jackson about that argument? Would he tell her the truth?

"We didn't find anybody," Patrick announced as he marched into the room with Gil and Marco.

"Neither did we," Gretchen replied. She left Jackson at the fireplace and plopped down next to Hannah on the couch.

"Did you check everywhere down here?" Jackson asked.

"Everywhere except the kitchen," Gretchen told him.

"Marco and I will do it," Jackson offered.

Gretchen watched Jackson and Marco disappear into the kitchen. She could hear them moving about. Then all was quiet. Minutes dragged by. Jackson and Marco didn't return from the kitchen.

Gretchen glanced at her watch. What was taking them so long?

"What's going on in there?" Hannah whimpered.

"I don't know," Gretchen answered.

She jumped up from the couch and strode to the kitchen door. She pressed her ear against the door. All was silent on the other side.

"The killer *is* in there!" Gretchen shrieked. "He's killed Jackson and Marco!"

chapter

19

"Jackson!" Hannah cried.

Gretchen stepped back as Jackson and Marco came walking out of the kitchen.

"What happened?" Gretchen demanded as they returned to the front room. She sat down next to Hannah. "What took you so long?"

"Sorry," Jackson apologized, sitting in a wooden chair across from the couch. "We were in the walk-in pantry."

"So the kitchen is safe?" Gil asked.

Jackson nodded.

"What do we do now?" Hannah asked. "Wait till the police arrive tomorrow?"

Marco shook his head. "No. We ask some questions."

Gretchen stared at Marco. "Questions? What kind of questions?"

Marco turned to Patrick, who was sitting on the floor in front of the fireplace. "How did you say you got that blood on your shirt?"

Gretchen watched as all eyes in the room locked on the front of Patrick's shirt.

"I told you," Patrick explained. "I cut my hand when I opened the bedroom window."

"But there isn't any blood on the windowsill," Marco said. "I know. I checked when we were searching upstairs."

Patrick laughed. "So? Is that supposed to mean I'm a killer?"

"Why isn't there any blood?" Gil asked.

"There isn't any blood on the windowsill because I cleaned it up." Patrick held up his bandaged hand. "And if you still don't believe me, you can take a look at the cut on my palm. Or check out the garbage in the kitchen. It's filled with pieces of broken glass."

Gretchen felt her body trembling. She knew it wasn't from the rain and cold, but from the fear in the room.

"Can we please stop attacking each other?" she pleaded. "It won't do us any good. Let's try to figure out what we're going to do next. We need a plan."

Hannah began crying again.

"I feel so awful," she sobbed. "I fought with Cindy yesterday afternoon. I found out she won the scholarship I applied for, and I said some horrible things to her. Now I'll never have a chance to apologize."

79

Gretchen studied Hannah, wondering if her tears were real. She remembered the scene in the kitchen.

Remembered Hannah saying she wished Cindy was dead.

Remembered how angry Hannah had been about the scholarship.

With Cindy dead, there was a good chance that the scholarship would go to Hannah.

And *no* chance of Cindy stealing Gil back.

Gretchen's eyes traveled from Hannah to Jackson.

Creepy Jackson.

Always staring at her.

Always watching her.

Could he have been watching Cindy the way he watched her? She hardly knew him. He could be capable of anything.

Even murder?

"I heard you arguing with Cindy tonight, Jackson," Gretchen blurted out. "I was outside. I heard you through the kitchen window."

"No way," Jackson denied.

"It was your voice," Gretchen insisted. "I know what I heard."

She saw Jackson's cheeks turn red as his temper flared. "Are you calling me a liar?"

Gretchen couldn't believe what she was seeing. Jackson was losing his cool!

"I never argued with Cindy tonight," he insisted. "You heard somebody else. Maybe it was Patrick. Or Marco."

He's lying, Gretchen thought. I know what I heard. Jackson was arguing with Cindy. He slapped her.

But did the argument spin out of control?

Did Jackson do more than *slap* Cindy?

Did he kill her?

And would he have killed me out on the porch if he knew I overheard his argument with Cindy?

And . . . could he kill again?

chapter

20

*B*eside Gretchen on the couch, Hannah continued crying.

"It wasn't me," Patrick protested. "I wasn't even inside the cabin. I went outside, too. I felt drowsy. I thought some fresh air would wake me up."

Someone is lying, Gretchen thought.

Jackson's voice was the one I heard in the kitchen. I'm sure of it. And when I left the cabin, Patrick said he wasn't going to budge.

As for Marco, he was outside with me. And Gil was with Hannah.

"Would you stop crying?" Gil snapped at Hannah. "You're driving me nuts."

"I'm sorry. I'm so upset," Hannah sobbed. "I can't believe Cindy is dead. Tonight was supposed to be such a special night. And now she's never going to have another birthday."

"You don't care," Gil sneered. "You were ready to scratch her eyes out tonight."

"That's because she was throwing herself all over you," Hannah shot back. "And you were encouraging her."

"I was not!"

"Yes, you were!" Hannah narrowed her eyes at him. "Did you really think Cindy liked you? She was just flirting with you to get back at me."

"Are you for real?" Gil shot back. "If it wasn't for Cindy's parents, she and I would still be going out together. You're jealous. You were always jealous of her."

"Stop it!" Gretchen cried. "Before you both say something you'll regret."

Hannah ignored Gretchen's advice. She jumped off the couch and stood in front of Gil.

"Cindy didn't care about you," she told him. "If she cared anything at all about you, she wouldn't have dumped you."

"That's not true!"

Hannah nodded. "Yes, it is. Cindy always wanted what she couldn't have. She always had to steal things from other people. That's why she was always flirting with you. All that mattered was stealing you away from me."

"She didn't have to steal me away from you!" Gil screamed. "I was going to break up with you!"

"I hate you!" Hannah sobbed, tears streaming

down her face. "You're horrible! I wish you were dead!"

"Like Cindy?" Gil taunted. "With a killer on the loose, maybe your wish will come true. Maybe I'll be dead by tomorrow morning. Or maybe I'll get lucky and *you'll* be dead!"

Gretchen couldn't believe Hannah and Gil were saying such horrible things to each other.

"Stop it!" she cried, pushing herself between them. "Stop it! Stop fighting! How can you say those things when there's a murderer out there? How can—"

Gretchen gasped as the front door burst open. It slammed hard into the wall.

She spun around.

"Who's there?" she cried.

chapter

21

No one there.

"The wind," Jackson murmured. "The wind blew the door open."

Gretchen sighed. She had expected to see the killer standing in the doorway, waving a bloody knife, threatening to kill them all.

Jackson strode to the door and shut it. "I guess I didn't close it all the way."

Hannah sniffed. She sat back on the couch, drawing her knees up to her chest.

"The next time the door slams open, it could be the killer, getting ready to finish what he started with Cindy," she choked out.

"Why would the killer come back? Why would he come after any of us?" Patrick asked.

"Why did he go after Cindy?" Hannah demanded. She huddled in a corner of the couch. "All I know is that I'm scared. I want to go home."

"We can't go home," Patrick said. "Not until the police get here."

"By the time the police get here, we could all be dead!" Hannah cried.

Marco turned from the fireplace. "That's not very likely. We have a slight advantage. I mean, there are six of us and one of him."

"Not if he kills us off one by one," Hannah reasoned, wiping tearstains from her face.

"Hannah is right," Gretchen agreed. "I think we all need to stick close together. I don't think any of us should go off by ourselves. It's too risky."

Gretchen pictured Cindy's body sprawled in the flour.

What were Cindy's last thoughts before she died?

Gretchen gazed around the cabin at her friends. She felt as if she were seeing them for the first time.

She thought she knew them—but did she?

Could one of them have murdered Cindy?

Was that why Cindy's eyes were filled with such terror?

Had she been unable to believe that someone she trusted had killed her?

No, Gretchen thought. It can't be.

It had to be that escaped prisoner.

If he had been hiding in the Fear Street Woods, he could easily row over to the island.

It *was* the prisoner, she told herself. It *had* to be.

Because if it's not the prisoner, one of my best friends is a murderer.

Gretchen shuddered. "We're safer if we all stick together," she said.

"Yes," Jackson said. "We stay together at all times. Starting now. Follow me. We all have to go back to the kitchen."

"Huh?" Hannah gripped her stomach. "I can't even *think* of going in there again."

Jackson sighed. "It's important. I want to check out Cindy's body one more time."

"Why?" Gretchen asked. She couldn't help feeling suspicious.

"Maybe it will help us figure out what happened," Jackson replied.

Hannah shook her head furiously. "I can't go back into the kitchen. I can't!"

"Come on, Hannah," Gretchen coaxed, pulling her by the arm. "You know we're right. We have to stick together. You can't stay out here alone."

As soon as Gretchen led Hannah into the kitchen, Hannah raced to the other side of the room. As far away from Cindy's body as possible.

Gretchen saw her turn to the wall with her eyes squeezed closed.

Gil and Marco hopped up on a kitchen counter while Patrick leaned against the refrigerator. Ignoring the others, Jackson began walking around Cindy's body.

Gretchen stood in the center of the kitchen, inches away from the corpse. She stared down at the floor. She was standing so close to the body, her foot was practically touching Cindy's hand.

She noticed red nail polish on Cindy's fingernails, some of it chipped away. A gold charm bracelet dangled around her wrist.

But that wasn't all.

Gretchen's eyes widened.

How had she missed it earlier?

A baseball cap.

Gripped in Cindy's hand.

Cindy hadn't worn a baseball cap to the cabin.

If the cap wasn't hers, where did it come from?

Had someone else been wearing it?

The killer?

Did she grab it off her murderer?

Gretchen raised her eyes to the others. Jackson was watching her. She returned his stare.

"What is it?" Jackson demanded.

Gretchen swallowed hard to clear her throat. "Cindy is holding a baseball cap," she replied.

Hannah's eyes popped open. "What did you say?"

"Cindy is holding a baseball cap," Gretchen repeated. "She didn't wear one to the cabin."

Her hand trembled as she pointed to the cap.

"Who does it belong to? Whose cap is it?"

chapter
22

Patrick's mouth gaped open in shock. "It—it's mine," he sputtered.

"Yours?" Gretchen gasped.

Marco jumped off the kitchen counter. His eyes narrowed as he studied Patrick.

"How did your baseball cap get in Cindy's hand?" he demanded, narrowing his eyes at Patrick.

Patrick shrugged. "Hey, come on. Give me a break. I don't know. Why are you asking *me?*"

"Because it belongs to you," Gretchen said sharply. "You admitted it."

"Just because my cap is in Cindy's hand, you think I killed her?" Patrick exclaimed. "That's the stupidest thing I ever heard!"

Hannah's eyes shot to Patrick. She backed away from him. *"You* killed her?"

"Of *course* I didn't kill Cindy," Patrick insisted. He took a step toward Hannah.

"Stay away from me!" Hannah screamed. She darted to Gil's side. "Don't come any closer!"

"Hey—come on, guys!" Patrick pleaded. "You know me. We've been friends forever. Why would I kill Cindy? It's totally dumb."

"Then why is your cap in her hand?" Marco demanded again. "How did it get there?"

Patrick threw his hands up in the air. "I don't know!"

"Is that all you can say?" Gil cried. He had his arms around Hannah, who was shaking. "That cap is real evidence, Patrick. It points right to you."

"I want to go home," Hannah sobbed. "I wish we'd never come to this horrible cabin."

"It doesn't prove anything," Patrick insisted. "I don't know how my cap got in Cindy's hand. I hung it on the coatrack by the front door when we came in."

"Nobody saw you do it," Jackson told him.

"I am not lying! You *have* to believe me!" Patrick pleaded. "I hung my cap by the front door. Maybe Cindy decided to wear it."

Hannah uttered a bitter cry. "You're pathetic! Do you really expect us to believe that?"

"Cindy *is* wearing a jacket," Gretchen pointed out.

"You're right," Gil said. "It's my grandfather's lumber jacket. From the hall closet."

"So maybe Cindy was going outside for some air," Gretchen continued. "Maybe it was raining, and she didn't want to get her hair wet. So she grabbed Patrick's cap off the rack. Cindy freaked out if her hair got the least bit frizzy. Everyone knows that."

Patrick nodded. "That makes sense to me," he said.

"But if she was worried about her hair in the rain, why was she clutching your cap so tightly *after* she was stabbed?" Gretchen asked.

"I think she was trying to leave a clue to the identity of her killer," Marco said. "Maybe the killer was wearing the cap—and she pulled it off his head while he was stabbing her."

"No!" Patrick gasped, shaking his head. "No."

"You have blood on your shirt," Jackson pointed out.

"And Cindy is grasping your cap," Gil added.

"So what?" Patrick cried. "That doesn't make me a murderer."

"But it does make you look very guilty," Hannah blurted out.

"I have a gun—remember?" Patrick cried heatedly. "If I wanted to kill Cindy, I'd *shoot* her. I wouldn't stab her with a bread knife!"

Gretchen felt horror wash over her as she listened to Patrick's words.

She stared down at Cindy's blood-caked wound.

"How do you know it was a *bread* knife?" she gasped. "Tell us, Patrick—how do you know what kind of knife the killer used?"

chapter

23

"*B*ecause the bread knife is missing," Patrick replied. He pointed to the empty slot in the knife holder on the counter.

Gretchen's eyes moved to the tipped-over knife holder.

I'm becoming suspicious of everyone, she thought. I've known everyone in this room for months. And now I'm starting to believe one of them is a killer.

"I'm sorry, Patrick," she murmured. "We're all really scared and freaked out."

"Can you blame us?" Hannah cried.

"We can't accuse each other all night long," Gretchen added. She tried to make her voice sound normal. "We have to be calm and try to think clearly."

93

"And then what are we supposed to do?" Hannah demanded sarcastically. "Track down the killer? Give him a chance to kill another one of us?"

"What else *should* we do?" Gretchen snapped. "Stand around and cry? That's all *you've* done tonight."

The second the words left her mouth, Gretchen regretted them.

Hannah stared at her, mouth open in surprise and hurt.

"I'm sorry, Hannah. I know you feel bad about Cindy. We all do," Gretchen apologized. "I'm just really on edge."

"I think we all need to cool off. Why don't we head back into the living room?" Jackson suggested. "I think we're finished in here."

Gretchen followed after the others.

As she stepped around Cindy's body, she tried not to look. But she couldn't help it. She felt her gaze magnetically pulled down to the floor.

Cindy's blue eyes stared up blankly at the ceiling. Her mouth hung open in a silent scream. Bloodstains spattered the flour around her.

It's like a scene out of one of those slasher movies Cindy hated so much, Gretchen thought.

Gretchen felt dizzy. She leaned against the refrigerator. She pressed her face against its cool surface and took a deep breath.

When she opened her eyes, she felt better. She started walking again—but then stopped.

"Whoa! Wait a minute!" she called after her friends.

"What is it?" Jackson asked. He turned and strode back toward her. The others followed.

"What's wrong?" Jackson demanded.

"Look." Gretchen pointed.

Pointed to a dark splotch on the floor that looked different from the rest.

What was it?

Gretchen knelt down. She felt her pulse race.

A footprint?

No, that wasn't right. Not a footprint.

She saw a pattern.

A design.

It was a bootprint.

In the flour.

They all stared down at it. No one spoke.

Slowly, Gretchen guessed at what must have happened.

Cindy and the killer were in the kitchen. They were arguing. Cindy slapped the killer. He dove at her.

Cindy backed away. She bumped the flour canister and knocked it over. Flour scattered everywhere.

The killer stabbed Cindy. She fell into the flour, bleeding.

Then the killer walked away.

Stepping into the spilled flour.

Leaving a bootprint behind.

"Such a *clear* bootprint," Gretchen murmured.

"If the killer stepped in the flour . . ." Gil began.

". . . Then there would be flour on the bottom of his boot," Gretchen finished.

"I get it," Jackson said. "The bootprint will help us figure out who the killer is."

"We all suspect Patrick, so let's start with him," Marco urged. "Grab him!"

Gil and Jackson dove at Patrick. They each grabbed an arm, holding tight.

"Hey!" Patrick protested. "What are you doing?" He twisted and turned, trying to break free. "Give me a break, guys!" he cried. "Come on! Give me a break! Let go!"

"Go check out his boots," Jackson ordered Gretchen. "They should be by the front door with the others."

Gretchen hurried out of the kitchen and raced for the front door. Their hiking boots were lined up against the wall.

She searched for Patrick's boots. Hannah's had bright red laces, while Gil's laces were neon yellow. Jackson's hiking boots were black. Marco's were olive green.

Gretchen carefully picked up Patrick's boots by their tops.

She took a deep breath.

Was there flour on the sole?

chapter
24

Y_{es.}

A thin coating of white flour on the heel and sole of his right boot.

Gretchen gasped. The shock made her head spin.

She felt like dropping the boots on the floor and running out the front door.

But she took a deep breath, then studied the bottom of Patrick's boot again.

She didn't want to believe it.

She didn't want to believe that Patrick murdered Cindy.

Sweet, lovable Patrick. Always joking. Always kidding around.

He could never do something this evil. This wicked.

She didn't want to believe it. She liked him too much.

But there was no denying the evidence.

The blood on his shirt.

His cap in Cindy's hand.

And now the flour on the bottom of his boot.

Carrying the boots, she walked slowly back to the kitchen.

Everyone hovered in the doorway, waiting to learn what she had discovered.

Waiting to learn who the killer was.

Patrick.

Gretchen stepped back into the kitchen.

"Well?" Marco demanded. "What did you find?"

"There's flour on the bottom of one of his boots," Gretchen announced. She lifted the boot so everyone could see the flour on the sole.

Gretchen's gaze fixed on Patrick. She saw disbelief wash over Patrick's face. "I don't know how that flour got there. I swear it!"

"It got there when you murdered Cindy," Marco accused.

"But—I didn't kill Cindy," Patrick cried. "I swear it! You've got to believe me!"

Hannah slumped into a chair at the kitchen table and began sobbing again. "Why did we ever agree to come out to the island tonight?" she wailed. "We should have stayed in Shadyside. If we had, none of this would have happened. Cindy would still be alive."

"We don't know that," Gil stated. "If Patrick

wanted Cindy dead, he could have killed her any-where."

"I didn't kill her!" Patrick insisted. "The escaped prisoner did it. Gretchen, you believe me—don't you?"

Gretchen swallowed hard. She didn't know how to answer.

She wanted to believe Patrick was innocent. His pleas sounded so truthful and honest.

But all the evidence pointed to him.

"I want to believe you, Patrick," she whispered. "Really, I do. But I can't."

"What do we do now?" Gil asked.

"First, let's tie Patrick up," Marco suggested. "Then we can decide what to do without having to worry about getting killed."

He pulled open kitchen drawers until he found a coil of rope.

Gretchen stood behind Hannah as Gil and Jackson pushed Patrick into a kitchen chair. Then Marco wound the rope around Patrick's body.

"No!" Patrick protested, trying to break free. "This isn't fair! I didn't do anything."

"Don't hurt him," Gretchen begged, as Marco forced Patrick back down.

"We're not going to hurt him," Marco told her. "We're just making sure he doesn't hurt *us.*"

After tightly securing Patrick to the chair, Marco stepped back.

"Now what?" Gretchen cried.

"We search through his things," Marco replied.

"Why?" Gretchen asked.

"What's the point?" Hannah demanded.

"To see if he's hiding anything," Marco explained.

"You *can't* go through my things!" Patrick protested.

"Don't tell us what we can do," Marco snapped. "We're in charge. Not you."

"Go ahead," Patrick sneered. "Look through my things. You won't find anything—because I didn't do anything. You're wasting your time."

Gretchen left the hiking boots on the kitchen table and followed after Gil, Jackson, and Marco.

She paused in the kitchen doorway. "Hannah, aren't you coming?"

Hannah didn't answer. She slumped over the kitchen table, her head in her hands, her body trembling. She looked paralyzed with fright.

"Hannah, get up and come with us," Gretchen said calmly. "The guys need our help."

Hannah nodded. She stood up shakily and followed Gretchen out of the kitchen.

The front room was cold and dark. The fire had died down, and only a few candles were still burning.

Gretchen shivered.

Was it only a few hours ago that they'd been laughing and partying?

It seemed like a lifetime ago.

"I found Patrick's backpack," Marco announced, lifting it from behind the couch.

Marco opened the backpack and spilled the contents onto the coffee table. Gretchen saw a pair of white socks fall out first. Then a rolled up T-shirt. A pack of chewing gum. Patrick's toothbrush and toothpaste. Some loose change and a motorcycle magazine.

Gil, Jackson, and Marco sifted through the items. So far, nothing looked very interesting. Maybe they wouldn't find anything.

Maybe, despite all the evidence, they were wrong, and Patrick hadn't killed Cindy. Maybe he *was* telling the truth.

At the edge of the coffee table, Gretchen noticed a folded-up piece of paper that had fallen out of the backpack.

Curious, she picked it up and unfolded it.

She read the few words written on it.

And gasped.

chapter
25

She held out the sheet of paper to the others.

"You can stop looking. Here's all the proof we need," she declared. She heard her own voice tremble. "Patrick is definitely the killer."

"What is it?" Jackson demanded. "What did you find?"

"A note from Cindy to Patrick," Gretchen answered.

"Read it," Jackson urged. "Tell us what it says."

Gretchen cleared her throat and lowered her eyes to the note. She read:

Patrick, I can't keep our secret anymore. I'm going to tell my parents—no matter what happens. Don't try to stop me. Cindy.

Gretchen heard Hannah gasp.

What kind of secret could Patrick and Cindy have been keeping?

"Could something have been going on between Cindy and Patrick?" Gretchen whispered. "Without any of us knowing?"

"Why wouldn't they tell us?" Hannah asked.

"You know how strict her parents are," Gretchen reminded them. "Maybe Cindy didn't think they'd let her see him."

"Tell me about it," Gil muttered. "They didn't think any guy was good enough for Cindy."

Marco shook his head. "It can't be that. Even if Cindy didn't want her parents to know she was seeing Patrick, she would have told *us*. We were her best friends. It has to be something else."

"Like what?" Gretchen asked. She couldn't think of any other explanation. She felt so confused.

"Let's keep looking through Patrick's stuff," Marco urged. "We found the note. We may find something else."

Gretchen sighed and headed across the living room to the corner where the sleeping bags were piled up. She searched for Patrick's sleeping bag and found it on the bottom of the pile.

"This is probably going to be a waste of time," she said, pulling it out.

Gretchen unrolled the sleeping bag. "Oh no," she moaned. "Oh no! Oh no!"

Gretchen staggered back from the sleeping bag, covering her eyes with her hands.

Jackson rushed to her side. She felt his hand on her arm, steadying her. "What is it?" he cried.

Marco, Gil, and Hannah hurried over, surrounding her. "What's wrong?" Marco asked. "What did you find?"

Gretchen pointed to the floor.

There, in the middle of Patrick's sleeping bag, was the missing bread knife.

Its blade covered with dark stains.

chapter
26

"*T*he knife used to kill Cindy," Gretchen murmured.

They all stood staring down at the sleeping bag.

At the knife.

Gretchen's gaze fixed on the razor-sharp edge of the blade.

She shivered and tore her eyes away. The thought of the knife slashing into Cindy made her feel sick.

She hugged her arms around her stomach. And forced herself not to look at it again.

"I can't believe it," she heard Hannah moan. "I can't believe that Patrick . . ."

Gretchen suddenly felt light-headed. She staggered to the couch and sat down. She dropped her head down to her knees and swallowed deep breaths.

She heard someone walk toward her.

"Are you okay?" Jackson asked softly.

Gretchen pushed her hair out of her face. "I'm okay," she answered. "I guess."

"This is all the proof we need," Marco said. "Let's see Patrick try to deny this!"

Marco led the way back to the kitchen.

"I can't go back in there," Hannah whispered. She clutched Gretchen's arm. "Stay out here with me. Please?"

"I want to hear what Patrick says when he sees the knife," Gretchen told her.

She put her arms around Hannah and gave her a hug. "I'll come back in a minute, okay?"

"Okay," Hannah nodded. She twisted the bottom of her sweater in her hands. "I'll wait out here, by the door. I'll be okay."

Gretchen turned from Hannah and stepped into the kitchen.

Marco, Jackson, and Gil stood in a grim circle around Patrick.

"I knew you wouldn't find anything," Patrick said angrily. "Now untie me!"

"You're wrong, Patrick," Gretchen said. "We did find things. Two things."

All the blood drained from Patrick's face. His mouth fell open, and he stared at Gretchen as if he hadn't heard her correctly. "Excuse me?"

Gretchen stared hard at Patrick.

Either he's telling the truth and didn't murder

Cindy. Or he's giving the performance of his life, she thought.

"We found two things," Gretchen repeated. "We found a note in your backpack. From Cindy. She said she was going to tell her parents about the secret the two of you shared. She said she couldn't keep it anymore."

"I don't know what you're talking about," Patrick said through gritted teeth. "Cindy and I didn't share any secret. The note is a fake. It has to be a total fake. I never got any note from Cindy."

They all stared hard at Patrick, studying his face.

Patrick sighed. "What else did you find?"

Gretchen took a deep breath. "The missing bread knife . . . smeared with blood . . . in your sleeping bag."

"You murdered her!" Gil cried suddenly.

"I didn't! I didn't!" Patrick screamed.

"But Patrick," Gretchen cut in. "How do you explain the knife in your sleeping bag?" Gretchen asked.

"I don't know. I really don't. I didn't put it there," Patrick insisted.

"But it *was* there," Gretchen stated. "And it's smeared with blood."

"I didn't murder Cindy!" Patrick cried. "Why won't anyone listen to me? If you'd only untie me, I could help you figure this out."

"Save it," Gil ordered harshly. He moved closer to Patrick. "We're not untying you. We're going to hold you until we can get the police. When they get here, you can tell them that you're innocent."

"Please," Patrick begged. "You have to listen to me."

Gretchen shook her head. "There's nothing left to say," she told him. "There's just too much proof."

"That's the whole point!" Patrick exclaimed. "If I killed Cindy, would I make it so easy for you? Would I leave so much evidence around?"

Patrick's eyes darted frantically around the kitchen.

"If I was the killer, would I hide the knife in *my* sleeping bag?" Patrick demanded. "Would I walk around in a bloody shirt, and leave flour on my boots? Would I leave my cap in Cindy's hand? And leave her note in my own backpack?"

Patrick's eyes pleaded with Gretchen.

She suddenly felt uncomfortable.

Patrick's words made sense.

"Gretchen," Patrick pleaded, "you're the only one willing to keep an open mind. You know I couldn't have done this."

Gretchen swallowed hard and stared down at the floor.

"Please, just think about it," Patrick continued. "Somebody is trying to make me look guilty. I'm not stupid. If I were the killer, I wouldn't leave clues all over the cabin."

He let out an angry cry. "Don't you see? Someone is trying to pin the blame on me. It has to be one of *you.*"

Gretchen turned to the open doorway. She saw Hannah standing there. Their eyes met.

Sometimes I wish she was dead!

Hannah's words about Cindy echoed in Gretchen's mind.

"You're not going to listen to him, are you?" Hannah asked shrilly. "He'll say anything so we'll untie him. If we let him loose, we'll all be in danger."

"Don't you see what's happening here?" Patrick demanded. "Someone in this cabin is trying to frame me."

"Frame you?" Gretchen asked. "Why would someone want to frame you?"

"I don't know!" Patrick exclaimed. "But they went too far. They planted *too much* evidence! If I killed Cindy, I'd try to *hide* the evidence. I wouldn't leave it all lying around."

From his seat at the table, Jackson cast a doubtful look in Gretchen's direction. She could see the question in his eyes. He had his doubts, too.

Gretchen turned to Gil and Marco, sitting on the counter. Both looked uneasy. She could tell they were also unsure.

"He's right," Jackson agreed. "We've been stupid."

Gretchen didn't know what to believe. She paced the kitchen. She took Cindy's note out of her pocket and read it again.

She saw Patrick watching her, straining at the ropes to see the note. "Is that the note you found?" he asked. "Let me see it."

Gretchen stopped in front of Patrick's chair. She unfolded the paper and held it up in front of him.

Patrick leaned forward, pulling the ropes taut.

Gretchen watched as his eyes moved across the handwritten words.

When he reached the bottom, his mouth dropped open.

"I don't believe it!" he cried.

chapter

27

"*I*t's phony! A complete phony!" Patrick declared.

"How can you say that?" Gretchen asked him. "I've seen Cindy's handwriting hundreds of times. So have the rest of us."

"But it *isn't* Cindy's handwriting," Patrick insisted.

"It looks like her handwriting to me," Gretchen replied.

"Sure, if you look at it quickly. But you missed something," Patrick said heatedly. "Something that proves Cindy didn't write it."

"What?" Gretchen demanded.

"Cindy always dotted the 'i' in her name with a heart. Don't you remember?" Patrick reminded her. "Look at her signature. It doesn't have a heart!"

Gretchen flipped the note over and studied the handwriting. Instantly, she saw what she had missed earlier. No heart.

"He's right," she said. "The 'i' isn't dotted with a heart. And Cindy always did that."

"Let me see it," Hannah declared, walking into the room. "I was Cindy's best friend. I would know her handwriting better than any of you."

Hannah snatched the note out of Gretchen's hand. Her eyes traveled over it, and then she returned it.

"That's Cindy's handwriting," she said firmly. "Even if the heart is missing. It doesn't matter."

"But Cindy *always* used a heart," Patrick repeated. "She never forgot it."

Gil sighed. "He's right."

"Cindy and I didn't *have* any secret," Patrick insisted. "Whoever wrote this note was trying to frame me. But they messed up by forgetting to use a heart."

Gretchen passed the note to the others. Now no one was sure if it was Cindy's handwriting or not.

"Why don't we look in Cindy's bag?" Gil suggested. "Maybe she has something with her handwriting on it."

"Good idea," Gretchen agreed. "That way we'll know for sure if she wrote the note."

They hurried into the front room.

"There it is!" Gretchen cried, spotting it under the couch where it had fallen.

Sitting on the couch, Gretchen pulled the black bag onto her lap and began emptying it out.

There wasn't much inside. Lip gloss. Eye shadow. A pack of chewing gum. House keys. A compact. Hairbrush. Sunglasses.

"Is that all?" Marco asked.

Gretchen scraped the bottom of the bag and brushed across a few scraps of paper. She grabbed them and pulled them out.

"These might have something written on them," she announced excitedly.

She unfolded the pages slowly as the others gathered around her. She looked down at the pages, her pulse racing as she tried to figure out what was written on them.

"They're notes," she murmured, scanning a list of names, dates, and places. "Notes from history class."

"Let's compare it to the note we found," Jackson urged.

Gretchen pulled out the note to Patrick. She placed it on top of the coffee table next to Cindy's history notes.

The handwriting looked identical.

Gretchen's eyes traveled back and forth between the two sheets of paper, searching for differences.

She could see that Cindy's history notes were written in a rushed, hurried style. But they were easy to read.

The note from Patrick's backpack looked neater. Gretchen had the feeling it had been written more carefully. The letters were crisper. More detailed.

But it was still Cindy's handwriting.

Except for one small difference.

"Take a look at the 'y's," Gretchen pointed out.

"What about them?" Hannah asked.

"The 'y's in the note from Patrick's backpack are different from the 'y's in Cindy's notes," Gretchen told them.

She felt her heart pound as she spoke. "Cindy's 'y's are loopy, but the 'y's in the note from Patrick's backpack have squiggles."

Gretchen set down the notes. Her hand trembled. "You know what this means," she said.

Marco whistled softly. "Patrick is telling the truth. Someone *is* trying to frame him."

"But who?" Gretchen whispered. "Who?"

chapter
28

She stared at her friends. All wore stunned expressions on their faces.

She thought she knew them—but did she? Could one of them have murdered Cindy?

If they were wrong about Patrick, then the killer was still loose.

A chill of fear swept down Gretchen's back. She shook it away.

I can't allow myself to be afraid. If I'm frightened, I won't be able to think clearly. I need to keep my wits, she told herself.

Gretchen took a deep breath. She folded the two notes and slipped them into the front pocket of her jeans. "We'd better tell Patrick what we found," she said.

Gil led the way back to the kitchen.

"Well?" Patrick asked. "Did you find anything in Cindy's bag?"

Gretchen nodded her head. "We did."

"And?"

"You were right," Gretchen told him. She pulled out the two notes and showed them to Patrick. "The note in your backpack was a fake."

"I *told* you!" Patrick exclaimed. "I told you I didn't murder Cindy."

"Well, we had to make sure," Gil grumbled.

"Don't you think we should untie him?" Gretchen asked.

Marco and Jackson began loosening the ropes. They fell to the floor. Patrick jumped out of the chair, stretching his stiff limbs.

"What do we do now?" Gretchen asked.

"We need a game plan," Patrick replied. "Why don't we all head back into the living room? I can't stand being in here with Cindy's body."

"Wait a minute!" Gil cried.

Gretchen spun to face Gil. "What is it? What's wrong?"

"Where's Hannah?" Gil asked.

Gretchen gazed around the kitchen.

"Hannah?" Gretchen called. She ran out into the hallway. No Hannah. "Are you out here? Answer me!" She darted into the front room.

Empty.

Gretchen turned as the others rushed in behind her.

"She's not in here!" Gretchen cried.

"I'll check upstairs," Marco said.

"I'll come with you," Gil said. They ran to the stairs, calling Hannah's name. Then they pounded up the short staircase two steps at a time.

Patrick and Jackson both wore grim expressions. Neither said a word.

"She's not up here!" Gil called down from the second-floor landing. He and Marco came running back down.

"Not upstairs," Gil repeated breathlessly.

Gretchen stared back at him. Unable to speak. Unable to move.

The choked words escaped her throat. "Hannah has disappeared."

chapter
29

"We've got to find her!" Gil cried.

He turned and ran to the door.

"Wait a second," Marco said. He caught up with Gil and grabbed him.

"We'll go with you. Just wait," Marco told him. "We need to think for a moment."

"Think about what? Hannah could be fighting for her life!" Gil cried.

He swung his arm and shoved Marco hard. Marco stumbled back until he hit the wall.

The others stared at Gil, stunned.

I've never seen him explode like that, Gretchen thought.

Gretchen hurried to get her jacket. She wanted to go out and look for Hannah, too.

On a small table by the coatrack, she saw a folded-up scrap of paper, propped against a lamp.

"Look!" Gretchen cried, and pointed at the paper. "A note."

She snatched up the note and unfolded it.

"What does it say?" Jackson asked.

"Read it," Gil urged.

"It's from Hannah," Gretchen told them. She read the note aloud:

I can't stay here one more second with a killer. I'm too frightened.

Gretchen dropped the note on the lamp table. She raced to the front door and yanked it open.

Outside, on the muddy path leading away from the cabin, she saw footprints.

Gretchen turned back to the others. "We have to go after her. She's not safe all alone out there."

"She didn't get much of a head start," Marco declared. "We should be able to catch up with her."

"Hurry," Gretchen urged. "It's raining again. Pretty soon her footprints will be gone."

Patrick, Gil, and Marco pulled on their boots and ran out the front door. Gretchen slipped on her jacket, then hurried to the living room where she had left her boots.

A jumble of thoughts raced through her mind. Frightening thoughts.

Did Hannah really leave because she was frightened? she wondered.

Or did she run away because *she* killed Cindy?

Hannah and Cindy were always so competitive. And Hannah had really resented and disliked Cindy. For so many reasons.

But enough reasons to kill her?

Gretchen couldn't believe she was thinking these things about her friend. Hannah wasn't a killer.

But Hannah had been so eager from the start to prove that Patrick was the killer.

Was it because Hannah had planted the note in his backpack? Had she planted the bloody knife in his sleeping bag?

Gretchen found her boots beside the fireplace where she'd left them to dry. As she tied up the laces, she felt someone watching her.

She raised her eyes to find Jackson standing by the couch.

Staring at her.

His intense stare frightened her.

She heard the front door slam. The others had hurried out.

I'm all alone here with Jackson, she realized.

Why was he staring at her like that?

Why was he moving toward her so steadily?

Why didn't he say anything?

Gretchen felt her throat tighten. She could barely breathe.

Her eyes darted frantically around the living room, searching for anything she could use to defend herself.

Her gaze fell upon the wood bin and the heavy pile of logs stacked inside.

I could pick up a log and bash it over Jackson's head if I have to, she thought.

She took a step back.

She wanted to put as much space between them as she could. And she wanted to get close enough to the wood bin to grab one of the logs.

But each time she took a step back, he took one toward her.

Jackson stared into her eyes.

"I guess you suspect . . ." Jackson said.

chapter
30

Gretchen's whole body shuddered.

Was Jackson about to confess to her?

"I'm going to catch up with the others," she blurted out. She brushed past Jackson, trying not to act afraid.

"Gretchen—wait!" Jackson called. "Please—let me finish."

"No. I—I have to go!"

Gretchen sprinted through the kitchen and ran out the back door into the rainy night. Once outside, she followed the trail in the mud left by the others.

Trotting hard, she turned—and saw Jackson chasing after her.

Gretchen pushed herself to run faster. She had to catch up with the others.

She'd be safe with them. Jackson wouldn't be able to harm her.

Her throat burned. Wet tree branches scratched her face. She raised her arms to protect herself.

She felt her boots slip on wet leaves and mud. And she stumbled.

She clung to a tree branch to catch her balance.

She heard the rustle and snap of branches as Jackson came closer. Then she saw his tall figure, quickly closing the distance between them.

She searched the dark woods frantically for the others, but she didn't see them anywhere. She called out. But the wind was howling, drowning out the sound of her voice.

No one knew she was in danger!

She scrambled back onto the path and raced through the woods. Sharp branches snagged at her clothes. But she tore herself free.

She spotted a clearing in the trees and ran toward it. At the end of the woods, she saw a hill ahead of her.

Breathing heavily, she started climbing. The hill was steep, covered with jagged rocks and patches of ragged grass.

She clutched the rocks for support as she clawed her way to the top. She heard her own breath coming in ragged gasps.

The sharp rocks cut her hands, but she didn't care. Jackson still came after her. She could hear his thudding footsteps below her on the steep hill.

Up above, Gretchen saw the top of the hill. With an extra burst of speed, she raced for the top.

Too fast.

She slid on tall, wet grass.

Slid and started to fall.

Down, down the other side of the steep hill.

Rolling now, rolling helplessly.

Bouncing down the mud-slicked hillside like a rubber ball.

Finally, she slid to a stop. In a cold, muddy puddle.

Gasping for breath, Gretchen sat up and pushed her wet hair out of her eyes.

Glancing around, she tried to figure out where she'd landed. Where were the others?

Slowly, she climbed to her feet. She took a step forward.

Then stopped.

She heard a shout.

Gretchen spun around to scan the woods. Where did it come from?

She heard it again.

There! At the top of the hill.

Gretchen raised her eyes.

Jackson.

At the top of the hill. He took a determined step toward her.

Then he started to run.

His hands shot up over his head. His mouth opened in a scream. A scream of attack.

ALL-NIGHT PARTY

He barreled into her before she could move.
They both toppled into the mud.
With a loud groan, he pinned her beneath him.
She couldn't get away.
He's going to kill me! Gretchen realized.

chapter
31

Gretchen shut her eyes. "Get off!" she choked out.

"I'm sorry," Jackson apologized.

Untangling himself, he scrambled to his feet. "I-I lost my footing. Are you okay?"

Gretchen opened her eyes and stared up at him in shock.

He doesn't want to hurt me? she wondered.

Jackson held out a hand, and she reached for it.

Gretchen rose shakily and wiped her wet hair out of her eyes.

"What is your problem? How come you ran away?" he demanded, breathing hard.

"I was scared," Gretchen confessed.

"Scared? Of what?"

"You," Gretchen whispered. "I thought . . . I thought you were going to kill me."

Jackson's eyes bulged in disbelief. "Huh? Why would you think something like that?"

"Because you're always staring at me! Watching me!" Gretchen cried.

"I don't mean to scare you," Jackson said softly.

"Well, you do," Gretchen insisted. She took a deep breath. "Why are you always watching me?"

"I just wanted to talk to you about . . . something." He lowered his eyes.

Gretchen felt totally confused. "What did you want to talk to me about?"

"I wanted to tell you that . . . well . . . I like you," Jackson admitted. "That's what I was trying to tell you in the cabin. But you just took off. I guess it was a stupid time to try to tell you," he added softly.

Gretchen wasn't sure if she had heard Jackson correctly. "Excuse me? Are you saying—"

"I've really liked you for a long time. Since you came to Shadyside High," Jackson blurted out. "But I've never been good at talking about stuff like that. By the time I finally worked up the courage to ask you out, you were seeing Marco."

"Why did you decide to tell me tonight?"

"I heard you tell Cindy and Hannah that you didn't want to see Marco anymore. So I thought, Cool, now I can tell her," Jackson explained. "Then when Marco showed up here, I got angry. Then so many awful things started happening . . ."

Jackson shook his head. "I wanted to stop being a wimp. And just tell you how I felt. I mean, in case anything happens to us."

Gretchen stared at him in disbelief.

Jackson *liked* her?

"Marco and I broke up tonight," Gretchen said. She didn't know why she wanted Jackson to know that bit of information, but she did.

His face lit up. "Really? Um, does that mean maybe you and I—"

"Why don't we try to get through tonight first?" Gretchen sighed.

He nodded.

"We should find the others," Gretchen suggested. She started back up the muddy hill.

Jackson followed.

Gretchen felt safer than she had since finding Cindy's body. At least now there was *one* person she could trust.

Jackson likes me, she thought. That's so weird.

Forcing thoughts of Jackson out of her mind, Gretchen concentrated on reaching the top of the hill. Because of the mud, they kept slipping and sliding. But soon she could see the top.

As they neared it, Jackson held out his hand to help her up.

Gretchen grasped it, holding tight as Jackson pulled her up.

"We made it," he said breathlessly.

Gretchen turned toward Jackson, about to reply.

But before she could get the words out, a scream of horror ripped through the night.

"It's Hannah!" Gretchen cried.

chapter
32

Gretchen froze.

The scream seemed to come from the cabin.

She and Jackson raced in that direction.

A second terror-filled scream cut through the night.

Don't let us be too late, Gretchen begged silently. Please—don't let us be too late!

Leading the way, Gretchen ran through the woods as fast as she could. She pushed away the branches whipping at her face and clothes.

She had to get to Hannah!

As the trees thinned out, Gretchen could see the outline of the cabin at the end of the trail.

And she could hear Hannah's screams.

She was still alive!

Gretchen's eyes searched the ground for a weapon

she could use against the killer. Spying a sharp, heavy rock, she grabbed it.

Gretchen raced out of the woods with Jackson behind her. She hurtled toward the cabin, expecting to see Hannah struggling with the killer.

Yes! Hannah! Outside the cabin. Twisting to free herself from someone's hold.

Who was it?

Gretchen squinted through the darkness.

Then she recognized Gil, holding Hannah's arms.

Marco and Patrick stepped up beside him. All three of them were trying to drag Hannah inside.

Gretchen watched as Hannah kicked and screamed. She clutched the door frame of the cabin with both hands.

Marco and Gil held Hannah tightly as Patrick pried her fingers free and shoved her inside.

She kicked out at Patrick.

Pain washed over Patrick's face as he clutched his knee.

Gretchen and Jackson hurried up the front path and into the cabin. They found everyone in the front room.

Gil, Marco, and Patrick had surrounded Hannah in a circle.

She sat on the floor. Her mud-spattered clothes clung wetly to her.

She gazed up at Gretchen with a hunted expression on her face, like a rabbit surrounded by snarling dogs.

"Why are you doing this?" Hannah shrieked. "I didn't do anything."

"When you and I went down to the dock to look at the stars, you left me. You said you were cold. You went back to the cabin to get your sweater," Gil remembered. "You could have killed Cindy then, Hannah. Then planted all the evidence to frame Patrick."

Gretchen turned to Gil. "Why didn't you say anything about this before?" she demanded. "Why didn't you tell us Hannah went back to the cabin?"

Gil shrugged. "I didn't think it mattered. I thought the escaped prisoner killed Cindy. Then I thought it was Patrick. But now I'm not so sure."

"I got my sweater. Then when I got back to the dock, you weren't there," Hannah cried to Gil. *"You* could have murdered Cindy and framed Patrick. Not me."

Neither Hannah nor Gil have alibis, Gretchen realized.

Either one of them could be the killer.

"If anyone in this room wanted Cindy dead, it was you, Hannah!" Patrick declared. "You *hated* her."

"I didn't do it!" Hannah cried.

"Then why did you run away?" Marco demanded.

"Because I want to go home," Hannah sobbed. "I'm scared and I want to go home. That's the only reason."

"We know the real reason you ran away," Patrick suddenly accused. "You were trying to escape. Because you killed Cindy."

Gretchen watched as Hannah's features hardened.

She wiped the tears from her eyes with her fingertips. She stared at Patrick defiantly.

A cold smile hovered on her lips, and her eyes narrowed.

"You're right!" Hannah declared. "I *did* kill Cindy."

chapter

33

"*I*'ve killed at least twenty people," Hannah declared. "Now I'm going to kill all of you. Then I'm going back to Shadyside and kill everyone there!"

Gretchen stared at Hannah in shock.

But then she realized that Hannah was being sarcastic.

"How could you accuse me of such a thing?" Hannah lashed out. "There's a murderer in this room. But it's not me." She put her head down and began sobbing again.

Gretchen ran her tongue over her lips while listening to Hannah. Her lips felt so dry.

Finding her purse on the coffee table, Gretchen opened it up on her lap and started searching for her Chap Stick.

She sifted through an open pack of gum, a roll of breath mints, a hairbrush and comb, a pink hair band, her wallet, and loose change.

She dug around the bottom of the purse, trying to find the tiny tube of Chap Stick.

"Hey—" she cried out as her purse fell off her lap. Everything inside spilled out, scattering across the floor.

Gretchen bent down to pick up the fallen items. As she tossed them back into her purse, she came across a folded note.

Curious, she picked the folded note off the floor and opened it.

She quickly scanned the written words on the crinkled piece of paper, barely reading them. It was an old note. She didn't even remember now why she saved it.

She started to put the note back into her purse, but then stopped.

With trembling fingers, Gretchen stared at the words again.

It can't be, she thought. I have to be wrong.

Gretchen read the note a second time, much more carefully, and her eyes widened with horror. She felt a chill run up her spine as she realized the awful truth.

I know who the killer is.

chapter
34

"Gretchen?" Jackson's voice broke into Gretchen's thoughts. "Are you okay?"

"Patrick—why did you do it?" Gretchen asked in a hoarse whisper. "Why did you kill Cindy?"

"What are you talking about?" Patrick demanded angrily. "I thought we settled this."

Gretchen gazed at Patrick with disbelief. He looks so innocent, but he's not.

Patrick is a cold-blooded killer.

He planned this to the smallest detail. And he almost pulled it off.

Almost.

Everyone turned to stare at Gretchen.

Gretchen shook her head sadly. She felt the words

stick in her throat. "You killed her, Patrick. And I have the proof. Real proof this time."

"Proof? What proof? Why do you think I killed her?" Patrick demanded. "Why would I do such a thing?"

Gretchen held up the note she had found in her purse. "This is a note you wrote to me, saying that you would bring the soda for the party."

"So?" Patrick remarked. "What's the big deal?"

"It's the same handwriting as the note that Cindy supposedly wrote to you," Gretchen announced. *"You* wrote that note, Patrick. *You* left it in your backpack."

"Are you sure?" Gil snatched the note out of Gretchen's hand. He examined it closely.

"Where are Cindy's history notes?" Jackson asked. "And the note we found in Patrick's backpack. Let's compare them to this note."

Gretchen reached into her jeans pocket and took out the notes. She handed them to Marco, and he spread them out on the coffee table.

Jackson and Gil sat down on either side of him and studied the notes.

"Gretchen is right," Marco said, looking up at Patrick. "The writing matches."

Hannah peeked at the note. "How can you tell?"

"Take a look at the 'y' in the note Patrick wrote to me," Gretchen explained. "It's written the same squiggly way as the 'y' in the note we found in his backpack. Patrick wrote both notes."

Patrick uttered a hoarse cry. "I wrote a note to myself? I wrote a note to make myself look guilty?"

He rolled his eyes. "Give me a break, Gretchen. I think you've really lost it now."

Gretchen felt the tension in her body pulling every muscle taut. Her head pounded.

"You know what you did, Patrick," Gretchen replied slowly. "You planted all the evidence against yourself. You framed *yourself*—didn't you, Patrick? To throw suspicion on someone else."

"Maybe I did," Patrick replied coldly.

He reached into his black leather jacket.

And pulled out the pistol.

"And now maybe I have no choice. Maybe I have to kill you all," he sneered.

chapter
35

*H*annah screamed.

"Put it down!" Gretchen cried. She took a step toward Patrick.

And saw him raise the silver gun barrel toward her.

Patrick shook his head. He stared at Gretchen with eyes that were suddenly glazed. His features were hard.

He's become a totally different person, Gretchen realized.

"Why did you kill her?" Gretchen asked. "Why did you kill Cindy?"

"Shut up, shut up, shut up!" Patrick chanted. He squeezed his eyes closed for a second, as if he were in pain.

"Everybody shut up. And keep still," Patrick

warned, opening his eyes again. He swung the gun around, pointing it at each one of them. "Don't move. I'm warning you."

"But why?" Gretchen insisted. "Why did you kill her?"

"Tell us," Gil said. "We want to know."

"She was your friend, Patrick," Hannah cried. "Why did you kill her?"

Patrick sighed. "She found out something I did," Patrick revealed. "Something bad."

"What?" Gretchen urged.

"Something that happened before I moved here," Patrick whispered. "No one knew about it. Not even my parents. But Cindy knew. Cindy found out."

"What did she do after she found out?" Jackson asked. "Did she threaten to tell other people?"

Patrick shook his head. "No. She didn't do that."

"Then what did she do?" Gil asked.

"She teased me," Patrick replied. "She loved teasing me about it. At first it didn't matter, because I was so crazy about her. But she didn't care about me. She didn't care about me at all! You know what she did?"

"What?" Gretchen croaked.

Patrick's face twisted with rage. "She pretended to like me. But she went out with Gil!" he screamed. "She didn't care about hurting me. She only wanted to tease me. All she cared about was reminding me about what I'd done. Teasing me. Teasing me. Teasing me."

He let out a sob. "It was too much. I—I guess I just cracked."

"And so you killed her tonight," Gretchen choked out.

"Yes," Patrick replied softly, lowering his eyes. "I—I planned it so carefully. From the moment I found out we were having this party."

His chin trembled. His whole body shook. "I gave Cindy a birthday present to die for."

Gretchen swallowed hard. I had no idea Patrick was so troubled, she thought. No idea.

I guess we never know what's really inside people—even our good friends.

"I almost changed my mind about killing her," Patrick continued. "After everyone left the cabin, I followed her into the kitchen. I told her I wanted to give her a kiss for her birthday. But do you know what she did?"

No one answered.

"She *laughed* at me!" Patrick shrieked. "She said she'd never let me kiss her. She tried to leave the kitchen, but I wouldn't let her. I grabbed her by the arm. And when I did, she slapped me."

So it was Patrick, not Jackson, I heard arguing with Cindy, Gretchen thought.

Patrick shook his head sadly. "She shouldn't have done that."

"Is that when you killed her?" Gretchen asked.

"Yes," Patrick answered. "You should have seen the expression on her face when she saw the knife. She really didn't think I'd do it. I didn't either. But—but I did."

Patrick's face darkened with anger. *"I did.* Don't

141

you see? I had to put a stop to the teasing. I couldn't take the teasing anymore."

Patrick raised the pistol and aimed it at Gretchen. His finger tightened on the trigger.

It's all over, Gretchen realized. Patrick's going to kill me.

"I'm sorry. But now you have to die, too," Patrick whispered.

Gretchen watched helplessly as Patrick's finger tightened on the trigger.

Squeezing it back.

There's nothing I can do, Gretchen thought. I can't get away. I'm going to die.

Gretchen squeezed her eyes shut. She covered her face with her hands.

She heard the deafening gunshot.

Then, her own terrified scream.

chapter
36

Gretchen waited for the burning pain.

Waited.

Waited.

She opened her eyes. She saw the front door of the cabin swing open. The door slamming against the wall had been the loud noise.

Not a gunshot.

A dark-haired police officer in a blue uniform stood in the doorway. A sandy-haired officer stood behind him.

"Are you kids okay?" he asked. He stepped into the cabin. The other officer followed behind, shaking rain off his uniform. "My partner and I—"

Gretchen watched in horror as Patrick turned the gun on the police officer.

"No!" Gretchen screamed. "Patrick! No!"

Gretchen threw herself at Patrick.

She pushed him to the floor, pinning him underneath her.

Behind her, she heard her friends screaming.

The two police officers dove across the living room.

Gretchen clawed at the gun in Patrick's hand.

He tried to twist away from her. Raised the gun toward her again.

Gretchen gripped his hand and smashed it against the floor.

Smashed it hard. Again. Again.

Finally, his grip loosened.

The dark-haired officer reached down and snatched the gun away from Patrick.

The other officer pulled Gretchen to her feet.

Patrick sprawled on the floor, rubbing the hand Gretchen had smashed.

The officer locked the handcuffs around Patrick's wrists.

Gretchen glanced at the nametag on the policeman's uniform: READE. "You got here just in time, Officer Reade," she told him.

"Looks that way," he replied, glancing around the cabin.

Gretchen took a deep breath. "He—he killed Cindy," she stammered. "Her body—it's in the kitchen."

"He stabbed her to death with a knife," Hannah sobbed.

"At first we thought the escaped prisoner had killed her . . ." Gretchen continued.

"Escaped prisoner?" Officer Reade gave Gretchen a puzzled look.

He pulled Patrick to his feet. Gretchen saw the dark scowl on Patrick's face. He staggered forward, his head hanging, his hands clasped behind his back.

"What escaped prisoner?" Officer Reade asked.

"The one who killed those three teenage girls," Gretchen replied.

The police officers exchanged confused glances.

"Officer Harding and I don't know anything about an escaped prisoner," Officer Reade replied.

Patrick tossed back his head in an ugly laugh. "That's right," he said. "There was no escaped prisoner. I made him up and told you he killed teenage girls so that you would believe he killed Cindy."

"And we did believe you," Gretchen sighed. "Because you were our friend."

"You were all so stupid," Patrick murmured, shaking his head. "You believed everything I told you. You fell for all the evidence I planted. The forged note. The bootprint in the flour. The bloody knife in my sleeping bag. Even with Cindy's blood on my shirt and my baseball cap in her hand, you believed that I didn't do it."

"That's because we didn't want to believe you could do something so horrible," Gretchen said in a whisper.

Patrick narrowed his eyes at the two officers. "Why are you here?"

"Your father told us you stole his gun. He said you were coming here for a party and asked us to get it back," Officer Reade answered.

"Patrick said that Cindy found out something about him," Gretchen told the officers. "She found out something he did before he moved here. Patrick said that's why he had to kill her."

Officer Harding turned to Patrick. "Oh, yeah? Did she find out you set that fire in Waynesbridge?"

Patrick sneered. "I don't know what you're talking about."

The police officers exchanged glances. "You got away with those things because of your father," Officer Reade told Patrick. "But you won't get away with this."

He dragged Patrick out of the cabin.

Officer Harding turned to Gretchen and her friends. "Do you mind waiting here until we take him back to shore? We'll send another boat back for the rest of you."

Gretchen watched until the officers were out of sight, then turned to her friends.

"How did Cindy find out that Patrick set a fire in Waynesbridge?" she asked.

"She *didn't* find out," Hannah replied. "Cindy didn't know anything bad about Patrick. She just liked to tease him. She used to tell him he looked dangerous."

"Dangerous? That's all?" Marco exclaimed.

"That's all," Hannah said sadly. "She didn't really know anything. Not anything at all. And do you know what I think? Do you know why Cindy teased Patrick so much? Because she liked him."

Gretchen sighed, suddenly feeling very tired.

Jackson slid his arm around her shoulders.

She snuggled her head against him.

Outside the window, the sun was rising.

"Party's over," she whispered.

About the Author

R.L. Stine invented the teen horror genre with Fear Street, the bestselling teen horror series of all time. He also changed the face of children's publishing with the mega-successful Goosebumps series, which *Guinness World Records* cites as the Best-Selling Children's Books ever, and went on to become a worldwide multimedia phenomenon. The first two books in his new series Mostly Ghostly, *Who Let the Ghosts Out?* and *Have You Met My Ghoulfriend?* are *New York Times* bestsellers. He's thrilled to be writing for teens again in the brand-new Fear Street Nights books.

R.L. Stine has received numerous awards of recognition, including several Nickelodeon Kids' Choice Awards and Disney Adventures Kids' Choice Awards, and he has been selected by kids as one of their favorite authors in the National Education Association Read Across America. He lives in New York City with his wife, Jane, and their dog, Nadine.

DEAR READERS,

WELCOME TO FEAR STREET—WHERE YOUR WORST NIGHTMARES LIVE! IT'S A TERRIFYING PLACE FOR SHADYSIDE HIGH STUDENTS—AND FOR YOU!

DID YOU KNOW THAT THE SUN NEVER SHINES ON THE OLD MANSIONS OF FEAR STREET? NO BIRDS CHIRP IN THE FEAR STREET WOODS. AND AT NIGHT, EERIE MOANS AND HOWLS RING THROUGH THE TANGLED TREES.

I'VE WRITTEN NEARLY A HUNDRED FEAR STREET NOVELS, AND I AM THRILLED THAT MILLIONS OF READERS HAVE ENJOYED ALL THE FRIGHTS AND CHILLS IN THE BOOKS. WHEREVER I GO, KIDS ASK ME WHEN I'M GOING TO WRITE A NEW FEAR STREET TRILOGY.

WELL, NOW I HAVE SOME EXCITING NEWS. I HAVE WRITTEN A BRAND-NEW FEAR STREET TRILOGY. THE THREE NEW BOOKS ARE CALLED FEAR STREET NIGHTS. THE SAGA OF SIMON AND ANGELICA FEAR AND THE UNSPEAKABLE EVIL THEY CAST OVER THE TEENAGERS OF SHADYSIDE WILL CONTINUE IN THESE NEW BOOKS. YES, SIMON AND ANGELICA FEAR ARE BACK TO BRING TERROR TO THE TEENS OF SHADYSIDE.

FEAR STREET NIGHTS IS AVAILABLE NOW. . . . DON'T MISS IT. I'M VERY EXCITED TO RETURN TO FEAR STREET—AND I HOPE YOU WILL BE THERE WITH ME FOR ALL THE GOOD, SCARY FUN!

RL Stine

I felt cold, hard bony fingers tighten around my neck. I fell to the ground, twisting and thrashing, trying to squirm away, trying to fight it off. But my whole body was heavy with panic. And I couldn't breathe . . . couldn't breathe. . . .

Beside me, I saw Jamie—eyes wide, mouth locked in a wide O of horror—being strangled . . . strangled by the skeleton, a hideous grin on the dirt-caked skull.

The strong, bony hands tightened around my throat and squeezed.

Twisting to pull free, I felt something drop onto my back. And then something hit my shoulders. I saw dirt flying . . . dirt falling into the hole. Falling on my head, my back. . . .

I couldn't breathe . . . couldn't breathe at all.

The dirt fell into the hole from above.

And over the roar, I heard that ghostly woman's voice: *"You'll pay . . . you'll ALL pay now . . ."*

The mountain of dirt was flying, flying and falling, filling up the hole again.

The two skulls grinned. The hard, bony hands tightened and squeezed.

And the dirt rained down.

My last thought: Jamie and I . . . no one will find us.

No one will ever know where we are.

We are being strangled—and buried alive!

FEAR STREET® —

WHERE YOUR WORST NIGHTMARES LIVE

R.L. STINE
FEAR STREET
ALL-NIGHT PARTY

R.L. STINE
FEAR STREET
THE CONFESSION

R.L. STINE
FEAR STREET
FIRST DATE

R.L. STINE
FEAR STREET
KILLER'S KISS

R.L. STINE
FEAR STREET
THE PERFECT DATE

R.L. STINE
FEAR STREET
THE RICH GIRL

R.L. STINE
FEAR STREET
SECRET ADMIRER

R.L. STINE
FEAR STREET
THE STEPSISTER

— COMING SOON —

By bestselling author

R.L. STINE

Published by Simon & Schuster
FEAR STREET is a registered trademark of Parachute Press, Inc.